THE LOST JOURNAL

CHRIS BLEWITT

Cover Designed by Jason Merrick

Bekitt Publishing 2012

First Edition

PROLOGUE

In a tent made of shabby cloth and single-braided rope, the General contemplated the difficult decision he was about to make. Only days earlier, the battle was being won, a new order was being formed and finally, peace had been restored to his land. He was tired, his uniform soiled and tarnished from months of battle, and he just wanted to see his family again.

The General did not acknowledge the four men who had entered the tent just yet. He raised the stone beer stein to his lips and took a long swallow of the dark ale. He wasn't caught off guard and didn't defend himself when they entered. He was alerted by his men that the enemy was coming, but he told them to stand down. Better to negotiate than to fight. At least, this time. The dark ale he drank, porter as it had become known, was cold on that dreary, gray afternoon. His men had just completed barreling the brew and he was the first to taste it. *Not bad*, he thought, although a little too much spruce. It needed time to age.

The tent was one of hundreds; each positioned approximately six feet apart on the hills of the Schukyill River. The General's Quarters were not far away, but he preferred to spend time in the field with his men. A small fire burned outside where a few men huddled around, warming themselves.

The General didn't offer a drink to his new guests, nor did he offer them a seat. He took the paper that was handed to him and read it slowly to himself. None of it came as a surprise. He'd written the document and all of its intricacies, fine details, and provisions in case the other side did not deliver as promised. He reflected back to the past few years and wondered if it had all been worth it. Should he press forward and continue the battle? He looked outside at the men in his regime: tired, beaten, cold, and hungry. They served him well, but to continue?

That would be impossible.

If he could save the country he'd spent his life defending and free her from the enemy, it would be his greatest triumph yet. That meant more to him. He grabbed the quill out of the man's hand and signed his name on both copies.

CHAPTER 1

The dark SUV pulled to the curb across the street from the house where Seth Layton had entered. It was a standard three bedroom suburban house built in the late 1950's. Cream colored vinyl siding framed a black shingled roof, and a swing occupied one end of a wooden porch. Seth had taken a few moments to find the correct key to unlock the door. He hadn't been to the house in almost a year and never once needed a key to get inside. Seth always knocked twice, and if the door was open, he let himself in.

Once inside, he let the screen door bang shut and left the heavy storm door open. Seth tossed the keys on the small table next to the door and took in his surroundings. No one had been to the house since his grandfather left over six months ago. Now it was his job to start cleaning the house and getting it ready to be put on the market. His grandfather was not coming back anytime soon. The living room to his right held a small couch and leather recliner. Both faced a TV that dated at least twenty years. It was one of those TV consoles that was twice as big as it needed to be on which people placed flowers or pictures on the top and definitely not HD compatible. Seth had spent many a night watching the Phillies on that TV, curled up on the couch while his grandfather, or Granddad, as he was called, sat in the recliner, hoping for a Phillies victory.

Seth went through the dining room and into the kitchen. He had a lot of work ahead of him. He'd contemplated whether to hold a yard sale or put everything on Craigslist. That would've meant too many pictures to take and upload, so he decided on a yard sale which was to take place the following morning. He took the day off from his job as a mortgage broker to tag everything in the house. The yard sale was listed in the local paper, and he had made a couple of signs to put on both sides of the street.

He went back out to the car to get his overnight bag and almost came to a stop as he walked down the few steps toward the driveway. Across the street in a SUV, he swore he saw a man in sunglasses put the passenger window up. He walked toward the driveway and let his gaze drift to the SUV as he walked. No movement, no sound, nothing. Why was a man sitting across the street from the house? Now that he thought about it, it had to be two men, one in the drivers' seat too. If they thought the yard sale was that day, why didn't they come to the door?

Seth grabbed his bag from the backseat and went back into the house, this time shutting the storm door and locking it. He peeked through the living room curtains; the SUV was gone. He was relieved and almost felt silly as he thought about two men watching his granddads' house.

The phone vibrated in his pocket startling him. "Hey Dad."

"Seth, how's it going? Did you get to the house yet?"

"Yeah, I just got here now. I forgot how much stuff is still here."

"You can take some stuff for your place you know."

Seth looked around at the outdated furniture. "I'm good, but if I see anything I'll take it with me."

"Sorry I couldn't help you but it's the club championship this weekend."

Poor excuse, Seth thought. His dad lived in St Augustine, Florida, miles away from Philadelphia. He moved down there after Seth's mother died three years earlier, and since he only worked part-time as a consultant for an airline, Seth's dad spent most of his time on the golf course. "It's fine, I can handle it."

"I appreciate it, let me know how it goes tomorrow," his dad said.

"Okay, I will."

"Oh and Seth, don't forget to check the attic. Remember how to get up there?"

Seth had forgotten the house even had an attic. He'd only been up once as a teenager to help get Christmas decorations down. The attic wasn't where most attic entrances were. To get there, he had to go through the master bedroom and into a small closet. From there he had to find the small entrance in the side of the wall, not in the ceiling.

"Oh yeah, I forgot about the attic. Is there anything up there?" Seth asked.

"I'm sure there's a few things people would want to buy."

"I'll take care of it. I'll call you tomorrow after the first day of the sale." Seth hoped to sell most of the things on Saturday and not have to lug everything out on Sunday too.

"Sounds good. Thanks again, son."

Seth hung up the phone and went upstairs to the bedroom closet to locate the entrance to the attic. It took him a few moments to pull back the rack of musty clothes and find the small cutout in the wall. To any other person, the attic would be impossible to find. It was a three foot by two foot cutout in the wall with a tiny space to slip your fingers in and pry the piece of drywall out. Seth squeezed through the small entrance and felt around for a light switch on the wall. He couldn't find the switch, but his head bumped into a string hanging from the ceiling and he pulled it until the light came on. In front of him were five wooden stairs that led up to another small door in the ceiling. Seth climbed the steps, pushed open the hatch, stepped up into the dark attic. He found another light and turned it on, illuminating the attic.

The floor was covered with plywood. Seth walked across the wooden beams to a stack of ten cardboard boxes. One by one, he opened each box and fished through its contents. He found a dozen things that he would take downstairs to sell. When he was finished, he walked around the small space to ensure he didn't miss anything. He was about to turn the light off when he stepped over a spot on the floor that seemed loose. Seth bent down and noticed a small cutout in the plywood about the size of a deck of cards. He pried out the small piece of wood and peered inside the dark space.

At first he couldn't see anything so he reached his hand in and felt around. His hand landed on a small metallic box that was tucked inside the pink insulation. He pulled the box out and stared at it. It was the size of a matchbook with a clasp on the front. Seth opened the box. Inside was a key attached to a small chain. It wasn't an ordinary house key, it only had two grooves on it and the number 641 was imprinted on both sides. He shrugged his shoulders, put the key in his pocket and went back downstairs.

Seth didn't notice, but the SUV was back outside the house a little farther down the street. Its occupants kept the windows up this time.

CHAPTER 2

The morning drew eager bargain hunters from all over the neighborhood making the yard sale a small success. The previous night, Seth stayed up until almost midnight pricing everything, and then woke at six to move everything to the front yard. The couches and bedroom furniture he left inside. He figured if anyone was interested, he'd bring them inside the house to look. He guessed he made almost three hundred dollars so far and that didn't include the two people that said they were coming back for the large pieces of furniture.

A male voice from behind said, "Excuse me, is this an antique?"

Seth looked at the item in question. It was a small chest, about three feet around, made of some kind of vinyl or leather.

"I'm really not sure," Seth replied.

He glanced at the man who held the chest and locked eyes with him. His face was small but chiseled.

He was in his mid-forties and had a clean-shaven head. Unlike the day before in the SUV, this time the guy was not wearing sunglasses.

"Hmm," the man said, "I'm looking for an antique, something really old."

Seth's fear of being watched was confirmed. Who was this guy and what did he want? "What you see out here is what I have to sell."

"That doesn't help me much. Maybe you have some books to sell?"

Seth pointed behind him and said, "The books are over there."

"I've looked through those books." The guy leaned in closer. "How about some really old books?"

Seth stepped back. "I only have what's out here, sir."

The guy smiled and laid the chest down on the table. He stared at Seth a few moments and then walked away.

"What was that all about?" a voice said.

Seth turned halfway around and saw a short blonde-haired woman walking around the table to face him.

"Huh?" was all Seth could manage. He was surprised at the woman's interjection, but when he got a good look at her, he was pleasantly surprised. She had sunglasses perched on top of her straight blonde hair and her green eyes locked on Seth's.

"That guy, what was he asking for, some books? Sorry, but I couldn't help overhearing the conversation."

"I'm not really, sure," Seth replied. "Is there

anything I can help you with?"

"Yeah, these two lamps," she said. "They're priced at ten dollars each. I'll give you ten for the pair."

Seth considered the offer but was more interested in her than the sale. He stole a quick glance at her left hand and noticed no ring on her finger. "I'll tell you what; I'll make you a better deal." Seth looked around at his dwindling yard sale and waved his arm. "The sale ends pretty soon and I could use some help lugging this stuff back into the house. If you help me wrap this yard sale up, the lamps are yours."

She smiled and contemplated his offer. "Let me think about it."

Seth was about to say something when she stopped him. "I'll be back in an hour if I decide I need the lamps." She smiled and started to leave.

"Wait, what's your name?" Seth asked.

She turned toward him and said over her shoulder, "Madison."

"I'm Seth, hope to see you again." He enjoyed watching her walk away in her tight camouflage pants and white tee shirt with a silver heart design on the front. He hoped to see her again.

The day came to a close and the only things that remained outside were a few books, a couple of small tables, some cookware, and of course, the two lamps for Madison. The large bedroom and living room furniture was still inside. At this rate, Seth felt he wouldn't put anything outside on Sunday. If the people didn't come back for the furniture inside, he'd put them on Craigslist.

His phone buzzed in his pocket and he picked it up.

"Hey dad."

"How'd it go today?" his dad asked.

'Good, most of the stuff sold," Seth replied.

"Great, keep the money. I appreciate you doing this for us."

"Dad?" Seth considered asking about the key he found or about the guy that came around asking for some personal books of his granddad's.

"Yeah?"

"Um, nothing, it's just that I may not have to do the sale tomorrow. There's only about fifteen things left besides the furniture in the house. I'm just going to put them on Craigslist."

"Okay, that's fine. I gotta run. Thanks again."

Seth wondered if his dad knew about the key he found but decided he should ask his granddad first. As the last of the buyers left the front yard of the house, Seth looked up and saw Madison walking down the street carrying a brown bag. He smiled. When she approached he said, "I saved the lamps for you."

Madison walked over and set the bag on the table. "I kind of figured you would. Want a beer?" She reached into the bag and pulled out two Sierra Nevada's and handed him one. I figured your refrigerator was empty."

"Thanks. You must live nearby, I didn't see you pull up in a car."

"Yeah, I live about two blocks away. I've never seen you around so I take it this isn't your house?"

"No, it was my grandfather's," Seth replied. "He's in a home in Malvern. He started losing it about a year or two ago and he wasn't able to live on his own. I'm really his only family around here, so it's my job to get the house ready for sale."

Madison changed the subject. "Alright, what do you need me to do to get those lamps?"

"If you could just give me a hand bringing this stuff back inside, the lamps are yours. Thanks for the beer, are you hungry? We could order pizza."

She shrugged her shoulders. "Sounds good." She took a long swallow of beer and set it down on the table. Seth grabbed a pile of books and went inside the house to order the pizza. Madison folded up a small card table and followed him inside.

After about thirty minutes, the front yard was clear and the pizza had arrived. Seth sat on the couch, Madison took the recliner and they ate their pizza. He found out that she worked at the bank a few blocks away. Most of her family lived across the Delaware River in New Jersey. The Phillies game was on the TV in the background and they led 4-1 over the New York Mets in the fifth inning.

After the pizza was finished Madison got up from the chair. "Well, I better get going,"

Seth was disappointed but didn't want to ask her to stay longer since they'd just met. "Oh, okay," he said.

"Thanks for the pizza," she said.

"No problem, thanks for your help."

She grabbed the two lamps from the floor. "Thanks for these too."

"Anything else you're interested in you can have," Seth said.

She looked at the old couch and chair and smiled. "I don't think these would fit in my place."

Seth laughed and said, "I don't blame you." He followed her to the door. There was an awkward silence. "Well, I guess maybe I'll see you around. Tomorrow I'll probably be around cleaning out the house."

"Okay," Madison said. "See ya."

He watched her walk down the front steps and saw her turn at the sidewalk and continue down the street. He'd forgotten to get a phone number, but at least he knew where she worked. Seth went back inside, finished off his beer and opened another one. He sat back down on the couch and watched the rest of the Phillies game. After some thought he decided the next day he would pay his granddad a visit. He needed to know about the key in the attic.

CHAPTER 3

After a long day and a full stomach, Seth had crashed on the couch and awoke early the next morning with the TV still on. He hopped in the shower and was out the door in less than thirty minutes. He stopped at the local convenience store, Wawa, and grabbed a cup of a coffee and a muffin. When he walked out of the store and back into his car, he saw the SUV again, idling across the street. The window was up and the glass was tinted making it impossible for him to see inside.

Seth made a decision: he would not be followed to his granddad's nursing home. He backed his car out of the lot and drove past the SUV going the opposite way. He almost cursed them out his window when he passed, but instead, he stuck his middle finger up. At the next street, he turned left and checked his rearview mirror. The SUV pulled a u-turn.

His car, a black Chrysler Sebring, was certainly not the fastest car on the street, but he thought he could make quick turns better than the SUV. At the next street he made a right-hand turn, then another at the next street. He then made a left and was back on the main road where he could pick up speed. A couple of cars filed in behind, and he didn't see the SUV trailing him. The nursing home was still fifteen minutes away and he knew a lot of back roads to get there. At the next major intersection he turned off and decided not to take the freeway. Still no sign of the SUV, he was in the clear, for now.

Harper's Grove Retirement Home was twenty miles outside Philadelphia, located three hundred yards down a narrow tree-lined street. Once you reached the end of the road a large courtyard was revealed, complete with stone statues and water fountains. Beautifully manicured grass, hedges and flowers covered the landscape. A circular driveway led to a four-story building. Seth drove his car around to the front and continued to the left of the building where staff and guests parked their cars. He never saw the SUV again but that still didn't convince him they weren't out there looking for him.

He got out of the Sebring and moved to the building's side entrance. There was a buzzer on the door. He pressed it twice.

"Name of guest please?" came the response.

"Arthur Layton," Seth replied.

"And your name?"

"Seth Layton."

After a moment or two, Seth heard a click on the door and pulled it open. He walked down a small hallway with no doors on either side into a large reception area. The first time Seth had been there was when he and his father dropped off his granddad a year earlier, and the last time had been about four months ago over Christmas. He felt guilty not going more often, but Seth was uncomfortable seeing his granddad in that position. When he was younger, Seth had gone fishing with his granddad more times than he could count. He played baseball with him and even taught him a little bit of sign language. He wanted those memories to last.

At the reception desk, he signed in his name and the time of nine-thirty. A male staff member came from behind the desk and said, “Follow me.” They walked down a long hallway and turned right at an intersection. It was like walking through a large hotel, room numbers adorned both sides. They got all the way down to room 1006 and stopped outside. The man knocked on the door three times and within seconds the door opened.

“Hi Arthur,” the man said. “You have a visitor.”

The door opened wider and Seth saw his granddad standing there in blue pajamas. “Hi Granddad,” Seth said. His granddad looked a little older than the last time he saw him. Seth couldn’t remember his age, but figured he was around seventy. He had a full head of gray hair and his face was droopy with two-day old stubble.

“Come in, come in, come in,” came the hearty reply from his granddad. The man with Seth walked away and Seth entered the room and closed the door behind him. The room reminded Seth of his college apartment at Villanova. The kitchen was simple, with a refrigerator, microwave, toaster oven and various cabinets and drawers. To his left was a loveseat, an arm chair, coffee table and a TV. His granddad took a seat on the couch and Seth sat down on the chair.

"How are you son?" his granddad asked.

"Good. I'm sorry it's been awhile since I was here last."

"Nonsense," he replied. "How are the wife and kids?"

A wave of confusion overcame Seth. Seth was not married, nor did he have any kids, but if he corrected his granddad, would it embarrass him or should he play along?

"I'm sorry, Granddad, I'm not married. It's me, Seth, your grandson."

"Right, right, I was just kidding, Seth. Weren't you pretty serious with a girl the last time I saw you?"

Seth wasn't, but this time he played along. "Yes, I was."

Arthur grabbed the cup of coffee on the table and took a sip. "Can I get you some?"

"No thanks," Seth replied. Seth felt bad but wanted to get around to the purpose of his visit. "So, how are you?"

"Ah, Seth, this place is not bad. Play bingo once a week, play poker with the boys too. My back acts up now and again, and lately, these hemorrhoids have been bugging the crap out of me. I gotta go see Nurse Stacy twice a week for my cream."

That's just what Seth wanted to hear about, his granddads hemorrhoids. "The Phillies are looking good this year."

Arthur waved his hand at Seth and said, "They

won't win anything as long as Larry Bowa is managing that team."

Bowa hadn't been the manager in more than ten years, but Seth let it go. "So Granddad, I was cleaning out your house this weekend and I had a yard sale yesterday."

"You didn't get rid of my music player or my albums did you?"

"No, no, we still have them," Seth lied.

"Those are worth a fortune, son. Hang on to those; they'll pay for your kids' college education someday."

Seth had already sold the albums for a dollar a piece, but no one wanted the music player. Maybe he'd hang on to it. "Granddad, I was cleaning out the attic and—"

"The attic!" Arthur exclaimed.

Seth was confused. "Yes—what about it?"

"Oh nothing."

"Okay, anyway, I found something up there."

Arthur scooted out to the edge of the couch. "What did you find, Seth?"

"A key," Seth replied. He reached into his pocket and held the key out for his granddad to see.

"The key," Arthur said in a slow and deliberate voice. "The key," he said again.

"You know what this is for?"

"Can I see it?" Arthur said. He reached his hand out toward Seth. He took the key and held it in his right hand while his left hand cupped it so it wouldn't go anywhere. He sat for a few moments and then rocked back and forth slowly in his chair with his eyes fastened on the key.

"Son," he finally spoke, "this key has been missing for some time now. I thought I looked everywhere. But I guess…" he pointed to his head, "…you know."

Seth could see the pained expression on his granddad's face. He was not only getting old, he was losing his memory. He tried to console him. "That's okay, Granddad, that key was pretty well hidden. I just happened to get lucky. So, what's it for?"

His granddad's expression changed from happy to serious. "Did you tell anyone else that you found this key?"

"No, why?"

"Seth, tell me now or we both could be in big trouble."

"No, Granddad, no one knows about it. I didn't even tell Dad."

Arthur got up and started taking off his clothes. "We have to go get it now."

"Where? Get what?" Seth asked incredulously.

"The bank," replied Arthur.

"The bank? The bank's closed today Granddad, it's a Sunday."

Arthur stopped pulling his pants down and started to pull them back up. "Seth, can you come get me tomorrow? First thing in the morning?"

"Tomorrow? I have to work tomorrow. What's this all about?"

"Take the day off son, I need your help getting to that bank, and they won't let me drive."

"Not unless you tell me what this key is for," Seth said, arms crossed.

"You're just going to have to trust me," replied

Arthur.

Outside in the retirement home parking lot two men sat in the SUV, the passenger with a lit cigarette in his mouth. His cell phone buzzed in his sport coat and he reached inside to grab it. He looked at the display and immediately recognized the name on the caller ID. He showed the screen to the driver and answered it.

"Yes, sir," the passenger said.

"Did he go to the home?" the caller asked.

"Yeah, we're parked outside. He tried to evade us, but it was pretty clear where he was going."

"Did he find anything?"

"Not sure. He either found something or just wanted to tell the old man about the yard sale." He inhaled the last of the cigarette and tossed it out the window.

"Okay, stay with him and call me with any updates."

With that, the call was disconnected. The passenger stared at the phone a minute and then placed it in his pocket.

The driver, heavy-set with receding brown hair, looked over at his partner. "What did he say?"

The passenger stared out the window and pulled the pack of cigarettes off the dashboard. "Nothing. Just said to keep tailing him."

"For what?"

"I don't know, Pierce. Boss said to stay with this guy until he finds something old, something valuable to him. He said when he does, we'll know it."

CHAPTER 4

The next morning Seth awoke while the sun was still low on the horizon. He was exhausted from the weekend and had gone to sleep early in his own bed. After leaving his granddad the day before, he drove back to the house and started photographing all of the furniture to put on Craigslist. A couple stragglers came by to look at some stuff, but he only sold about $100 on the second day. Madison never returned to the house.

Seth's apartment was situated off the main road nestled among tall pine trees. There were ten buildings in the complex. His was one of the last on the first floor. It was a typical bachelor pad, one-bedroom, big-screen TV, limited seating and an empty fridge. He showered, made coffee, dressed and turned on *Sports Center* to catch up on the weekend highlights. It was too early to pick up his granddad since visitors were not allowed before 8 am, and besides, the bank didn't open until nine.

He gathered his keys and jacket and decided to grab a quick breakfast at the diner down the street. Outside his apartment was the SUV. *What the hell is going on?* Seth thought about approaching the car and finding out who was inside. Maybe nobody was or maybe it was a different car. His instincts told him otherwise. He was being followed. Whoever it was didn't appear dangerous, at least not yet. He eyed the vehicle for a few moments and then got in his car and headed toward Pop's Diner.

Media, Pennsylvania, the town where Seth lived, was about twenty minutes from Center City Philadelphia. He grew up there, went to school there and never left. He worked in real estate and made his own hours, so calling out of work wasn't a big deal. His granddad's house was about fifteen minutes away in Broomall. Before his mother succumbed to breast cancer, his family was close. After, his dad moved to Florida and his granddad moved into a home. Seth had a brother who lived in Dayton, Ohio whom he saw about twice a year. Phone calls were just about as infrequent. Thank goodness for email.

Seth pulled into the gravel lot of Pop's and looked into his rearview mirror but saw no sign of the SUV. The diner had been around for decades and served the typical diner breakfast. Seth sidled up to the counter and was greeted by a middle-aged woman with a pencil stuck in her dark hair.

"What can I getcha son?"

"Hi, coffee, tomato juice, scrapple, egg and cheese on rye, please."

One time during college Seth took his roommates

there and introduced them to scrapple. They didn't taste it at first, especially after Seth explained it was leftover pork products and cornmeal, but Pop's made the best. It was about a half an inch thick, crusty on the outside and smooth and creamy on the inside. Once they tried it, they were hooked.

Moments later when his coffee and juice arrived, the bell on the diner door chimed. Seth sat facing a large mirror and had a view of most of the restaurant. He looked up and saw the bald guy from the yard sale and another man walk into the diner. Fear and panic set in and his hands began to sweat. He grabbed the glass in front of him and gulped down half of his tomato juice. The men looked around and were escorted to a booth on the opposite side of the diner.

A few minutes later, the waitress brought out his sandwich and laid the check next to his plate. "Anything else today?" she asked.

"Sorry, can I get this to go?" Seth replied.

She gave him a look of disapproval but reached under the counter and handed him a Styrofoam container. Seth put the sandwich in the box and finished his juice. He laid a ten dollar bill and some ones on the counter and started to walk out of the diner.

When he reached the door his pace slowed. He glanced over at the two men. *What the hell do I have to lose?* He walked over and hoisted the Styrofoam box in the air. "Guess you won't be eating here, eh guys?"

Before the surprised men could utter a response he'd walked out to his car. He revved the engine and sped out of the lot, keeping a watch in his mirror for the SUV that was sure to pull in behind him. After a few quick turns he entered the main highway. He drove with his sandwich in one hand and held the steering wheel with the other. Before long he'd arrived at Harper's Grove.

He opened the front door and saw his granddad, fully dressed in khaki pants, a blue shirt and a navy sport coat, sitting in the reception area. He looked good for his age. Arthur still held on to most of his ashen hair and at a little over six feet tall, he moved with only a slight limp from the hip operation a few years back.

"Right on time, son," said his granddad.

Behind him a nurse strolled out with a clipboard in hand. "Taking him out today, huh?"

"Yeah," replied Seth. "Is that all right?"

"It's fine honey. Arthur is one of our better patients. He tells a few too many stories," she said softly, "some, a little far-fetched. Just make sure he takes his meds and have him back by five."

Five? Thought Seth. Quick trip to the bank should take an hour or so. What was he going to do with him all day? "No problem. You ready, Granddad?"

Arthur walked out the door. "Where's your car? I wanna drive," he said.

"Ah, granddad, I don't know," Seth said.

"Come on, son. I haven't driven in over a year, almost two years to be exact."

"That's my point, Granddad. Let me drive and maybe you can drive home."

"Fine."

They walked over to Seth's car and were quickly on their way. Seth glanced around the parking lot. No SUV.

With rush hour traffic it took Seth a little longer than he thought to get to Southern Penn Bank which was located around the corner from his granddad's house. The building was nondescript and sided in brick with two glass doors, one drive-through window and another ATM drive-through. Seth found a parking spot and they entered the bank.

A female teller sat there filing her nails waiting for her next intrusion. Seth looked around the room. To the left were four desks, two of them were occupied with staffers who pecked away at their computers. Seth recognized one immediately: Madison.

When Seth and Arthur approached she looked up from her computer, smiled and said, "Stalking me?"

"Maybe," replied Seth. "But first, I'd like you to help my granddad out. Madison, meet Arthur."

"Nice to meet you," Arthur replied. He held his hands in front of him, unable to keep them from twitching.

Madison just nodded her head and said, "What can I help you with?"

"I'm not sure, but he asked that I drive him over here today. Granddad, tell Madison what you need."

He reached into his pocket and pulled out the key Seth had found on Friday. "I'd like to access my safety deposit box."

"Sure, what's the box number?"

"Six, four, one," Arthur said.

She typed for a few moments and said, "Arthur Layton, 2115 Carmel Street. Do you have a driver's license on you?" She felt a little embarrassed, but Arthur surprised her.

"Sure," he said. He reached into his pocket, pulled out his wallet, handed it to her and then looked over at Seth and winked.

"Okay, perfect," Madison said while taking the license and comparing photo to name. "Let me just grab the other key and we'll go down to the vault. She got up from her chair and Seth admired her good looks. She wore a black skirt that crept above the knee and a gray sweater that tugged at her chest. A long silver necklace hung down from her neck with the infinity design dangling from the middle. Both he and Arthur followed her across the bank's floor to another door. They waited while she punched in a code which led them inside another room without windows.

"Right here is where we keep all the secondary keys to the safety deposit boxes. There are one thousand of them, but my guess is that only a couple hundred are in use. When we grab the second key, we log into the computer the date, time, and the person, or persons who are going to access the box." Madison unlocked a drawer from her janitor-sized keychain. After a few moments, she pulled out a key, walked to the end of the room and started typing on the small computer.

"Just wanna log this in," she said. A few moments went by and she said, "Huh."

"What?" Seth asked.

Madison paused and typed a few more keystrokes. "Arthur, it says that this box has not been accessed since 1987, is that correct?" Both she and Seth looked at Arthur.

He turned away from them, shrugged his shoulders

and said, "That sounds about right."

"Granddad, why the sudden interest in this key if you haven't been here for twenty-five years?"

Arthur didn't acknowledge the question or their stares. He simply waited for Madison to log the information in the computer and shut the drawer. She told them to follow her and they walked through another access door and down a set of steps. Once at the bottom, she typed in another code by the door and they entered a small room with safety deposit boxes on either side of the wall. She found box 641 and handed Arthur the key.

"Feel free to open your box and look at the contents for as long as you want. I must leave the room and give you complete privacy. See you upstairs, Seth," she said and smiled.

Arthur took the other key from her hand and waited for Madison to leave the room before walking to the box and carefully inserting both keys. As the keys entered the box, Seth grabbed his granddads' wrists and said, "Wait, are you going to tell me what this is all about?"

Arthur relaxed his grip on the keys, smiled, and said, "No. I'm going to show you." And with that he turned both keys and pulled the box out of the wall.

December 14th 1799

The old man lay dying in his bed. Technically, at sixty-seven years of age, he was *very* old for his time. He had lived a good life, he remembered. Tough battles fought, but he'd won most of them. His sickness came on quickly. Two days earlier he was at work on the farm and came down with the common cold which quickly turned into pneumonia. In the room were neither his wife nor his children, it was his nephew Bushrod, with whom he felt a blood-line bond. He had four adopted children, two who died at age two.

The old man turned his head to cough, then turned back to look in Bushrod's eyes. He saw strength, courage, and honor in the thirty-five year old man. They had spent many a summer together the past few years and the bond was immeasurable.

"It's almost time Bushrod, I can sense it."

"I understand, uncle," replied Bushrod. He got up from the wooden rocking chair and walked over to the dying man and held his hand. "You have taught me well. I am forever in your debt."

"Then do this for me," the man said in a quiet whisper. "Go out to the barn and in the last stall at the end, climb the rails and look in the loft. You will find something. Bring it to me."

Bushrod did as he was told and came back moments later holding a small leather satchel. "This?"

"Please, come hither."

Bushrod brought the man the small pouch and laid it on his chest. He suddenly bolted upright ɪrom a coughing spasm and had trouble getting his breath back. His throat was full of phlegm as he spoke. "Son, do you remember everything we discussed this past autumn? The war? The redcoats from The Revolution?"

Bushrod nodded at the man and awaited his instructions.

"Inside this pouch, for those willing, there is a way to discover what you and I have spoken about. I ask of this to you; never, ever let this out of your sight. Pass it along to family members and them alone. Is that understood?"

"Yes, uncle."

"Never use this information for yourself. Never go near it, Bushrod. It will only cause you great pain. Never destroy it either. Someday it may prove useful. Do with it as I have done with it. Hide it in a location that you and you alone know. Is that understood?"

"Yes, uncle."

"Good. Now go along. I don't want you to see me like this." The man had a brief coughing fit but lay back down and turned his head toward the window. "Bushrod, remember me."

"Of course, uncle."

Bushrod laid a hand on the man and closed his eyes for a silent prayer. When he finished his uncle had closed his eyes and was sleeping soundly. He grabbed the satchel from the man's chest and walked out of the room, closing the door behind him. Curious by nature, Bushrod opened the satchel and reached his hand inside. He pulled out a brown notebook, a little bigger than a deck of cards. His eyes grew big as he flipped through the pages, reading bits and pieces of this man's life and the secrets he held.

CHAPTER 5

Arthur had the small brown book in his hands and was holding it up to the light like he could see through it. He had taken it out of the safety deposit box without another word, gingerly handling the fragile cover and the pages it held. There was a smile on his face, one that Seth had not seen in some time. He didn't flip through it or open it, he just held it in his palms, like it was a newborn child.

"What is it?" Seth asked.

Arthur chuckled to himself and closed his eyes. "Seth, I have not seen this in twenty-five years. Then I remembered it and could never find the key. So I forgot about it again. Until now when you showed up with the key."

"Granddad, why was the key hidden where it was?"

Arthur face turned serious. "Did you tell anyone about this key?"

"For the tenth time, NO!"

"Good. Seth, a lot of people are looking for this and some will stop at nothing to get it."

Seth thought of the men following him and how the bald guy had asked about old books on Saturday at the yard sale. He thought of telling him about the men but decided against it. He still didn't know what was in the book.

Arthur lowered his voice. "Son, you will know in due time why this book is so precious and why no one must know we have found it."

"Well, aren't you going to—"

"No, I'm not going to tell you about it right now and certainly not here." Arthur skimmed the first few pages. Seth tried to peek over his shoulder and see what he was looking at. All Seth could see was the worn parchment paper and some handwriting he could not recognize. Arthur carefully closed the book, put it back in the box and locked the door with his key.

Seth was dumbfounded. "What are you doing? Let's take it with us."

"No, not here, not now. We will do that later."

"Why?"

Arthur ignored him, finished locking the box and turned toward the exit. He knocked on the door and Madison opened it from the outside.

"Find what you wanted?" she asked.

"Yes, my dear, we have," Arthur responded. They climbed the stairs and came around to Madison's desk. Seth and Arthur sat down in two red-cloth chairs while Madison took her seat behind the desk in a plush leather reclining chair.

"Mr. Layton, I must say it was odd that you haven't

visited that box in twenty-five years. Curiosity overtook me and I searched your account. Sorry, but I have that right. Anyway, lucky for you, you paid for the lifetime package. We don't offer that anymore, but back in the eighties, you could rent a safety deposit box for life for one thousand dollars. That's what you did, and you'll have access to that box until the day you die."

Arthur looked up at her with a look of concern. "Let's hope that's not anytime soon, my dear." He saw her scanning the computer and asked, "Has anyone else tried to access my box in the past twenty-five years?"

"I can't say for sure Mr. Layton, but we don't let anyone access safety deposit boxes without proper identification and the key they were given."

"Huh," was all Arthur said. He leaned in close and lowered his voice, "Listen, I need access to the box again."

Before he could finish, Madison said, "Sure, Mr. Layton, you can visit that box anytime you wish."

He shook his head. "No, I need access to that box without anyone knowing I'm looking in there. Does that make sense?"

Madison was confused. "Not really. Mr. Layton, we do not reveal anything about personal access to anyone's safety deposit box. There will be no public record of your visit today."

Seth was confused and chimed in, "Granddad, what are you asking here?"

Arthur leaned in closer across her desk. "I need access to that box after hours." He felt pleased with himself and confident in his request as he leaned back in his chair.

Madison reciprocated and leaned forward. "Mr. Layton, I'm sorry but we don't allow anyone in this bank after hours, not even the branch manager. The alarms are set on timers and we set them as we leave and there cannot be anyone in the bank or the alarms will go off. Why do you need access after hours?" She sat back in her chair and looked at Seth.

"Beats me," Seth said as he shrugged his shoulders. "He won't tell me anything about what's in that box."

"My dear, without going into specific details, there are certain people who want what's in that box. I need to look at what's inside and take it without anyone knowing I'm here. Who knows, there could be people watching us right now."

Seth fidgeted and thought about the black SUV that was probably parked outside the bank. Madison just stared at the old man. She hoped for a better explanation, but she never gone one.

"I'm sorry, Mr. Layton, there's nothing I can do."

Seth rose from his chair and watched his granddad stare at the young woman, hoping for a little compromise, which he never got.

"Very well, let's go Seth." He got up to leave and then leaned his arms on the desk and said, "I hope you know that you could be endangering the life of Seth here."

Madison raised her eyebrows at the thought of endangering anyone's life, but she didn't cave. She couldn't. Rules were rules, and there was no way she was letting anyone in the bank after hours. The two men said their goodbyes and headed out the door. As they approached their car, Seth saw the two men exit the SUV not parked far away. They walked over to Seth and his granddad and the bald guy removed his sunglasses.

"Find what you are looking for?" he asked.

Seth and his granddad exchanged puzzled looks.

Seth spoke first, "What are you talking about?"

"Didn't you tell your grandson what you've been hiding all these years, Arthur? What's in the box in the bank?"

Arthur turned to the man and said, "I don't know what you're talking about."

Baldie sighed. "Hand it over. Let's save us all a bunch of time."

"I don't have it. It wasn't there."

Baldie reached into his sport coat and pulled out a cigarette and lit it. "Who are you kidding, Arthur? I could pat you and the kid down—you want that?"

"Go ahead," replied Arthur. "You won't find anything."

Baldie nodded to his partner and he began the pat down, first with Arthur then with Seth. He went in pockets, under the arms, and between his legs, there wasn't a place he missed. He looked over at Baldie and shrugged his shoulders.

"Let's go," Baldie said. As they walked away, he turned. "We'll be watching, Arthur. You come to this bank again, we're gonna nail you." He put his sunglasses on and flung his cigarette in their direction before walking back to their SUV.

Arthur and Seth got in their car and started it up. Before backing out, Arthur turned to Seth. "What is going on here?

"Those guys have been following me since Friday."

"You've seen those guys before?" Arthur asked.

"Seen em? They've been at your house, then they followed me to a diner this morning, and I guess they tailed us here. The bald guy even came to the yard sale and asked if I had any old books for sale!"

"Why didn't you tell me? Gosh, we should have never come to the bank."

"Gosh is right! Now we may have endangered Madison."

Arthur turned toward his grandson. "You know her?" he asked.

Seth composed himself and responded, "Well, we met the other night at the yard sale."

Arthur's eyes lit up and he said, "Perrrrfectttt."

The two men retreated to their vehicle and once again tailed the Chrysler as it pulled out of the bank. It was getting old. The driver stayed too far behind the car and risked losing them.

"Step on it!" said Kohler.

Pierce did nothing of the sort. "Why? What's the point?"

"We got a job to do is why."

"I don't give a shit about this kid and the old man. We don't even know what they have, where it is, or why it's so important."

"Pierce, *I* could give two shits about what you want. All I know is that we were given a job to follow this kid until he found the book. Well, if it's in the bank, guess what? We found it."

Pierce still didn't accelerate to catch up with the fleeing Chrysler. It was now a good quarter mile in front of them. Kohler looked over at him and their eyes met. For a brief moment, it looked like Kohler was going to cave in. But he didn't. Pierce stepped on the gas and gained ground on the black car ahead. Kohler pulled out his phone and made a call.

"Sir? Yeah, we're back on the road."

"They didn't find it?" the voice on the line asked.

"If they did, they didn't have it on them."

"What do you mean?"

"We staked out the bank. When they came out we searched them and found nothing."

"How long were they in the bank?" the voice asked.

"Fifteen, twenty minutes."

"They found it, goddamnit. And you're sure they didn't have it on them when they left the bank?"

"No sir," Kohler explained. "We did a pat down in the parking lot."

"What are you nuts?"

Kohler was caught off guard as he spoke. "Sir, you told us to look for the book."

"I didn't tell you to pat down civilians in the parking lot of a public bank! And stop talking right now! Stay on them and update me later!"

Click

Kohler looked over at his partner who had the smallest inkling of a smile as he drove.

"Shut up and keep driving."

CHAPTER 6

After Seth dropped Arthur off at Harper's Grove, he drove back down to the bank but waited in his car instead of going in. He was observant of his surroundings and didn't see the SUV but knew they were around. Seth was now concerned for Madison's safety. It was bad enough his granddad was involved; he didn't want to get a woman he just met mixed-up in this. Around twelve o'clock, he saw Madison exit the bank and get into a white Audi.

Seth pulled out of the lot after her and followed Madison to a supermarket. He parked far away from her and went into the store. After a couple of minutes he spotted her near the salad bar, taking a carryout container and filling it with assorted greens and vegetables.

"Hey," he said.

She turned her head and almost dropped her container. "What are you doing here? You *are* stalking me."

"Just keep making your salad, don't look in my direction."

She ignored his request. "Why? What are you talking about?"

Seth looked around the store but didn't see the two men anywhere. "Listen, I can't stay here. I don't want to get you involved."

"In what?" she replied.

"Good question," he responded. "I don't know. My granddad won't tell me what's so important about the book in the box right now. He said we need to look at it together in private."

"Seth, what's with all this cloak and dagger stuff? You know that vault is private."

"I know, I know. You heard him though, if we're in the vault too long, whoever is following us will know that we read the contents."

"Someone is following you?" she asked.

"Yes."

"Who?"

"Another good question," he said. "I don't think my granddad is crazy. I'm leaning toward believing him right now, especially since I've been followed ever since I cleaned out his house."

"I sure as hell don't understand what's going on, but you must understand that I can't let you in the bank after hours."

They both filled up on meats and cheeses and then added dressing, Lite Italian for her, Blue Cheese for him. Seth topped his salad off with bacon bits, Madison with sunflower seeds.

"There has to be a way for us to look at it without anyone knowing," Seth said.

She thought for a moment before saying, "I can get it for you."

"What? No, I told you I don't want you involved."

"Seth, if they're following you, they're certainly not keeping tabs on me."

"Not yet at least," was all Seth could muster up.

Now it was her time to lower her voice. "Just give me the key and I'll bring it to you."

"How?"

"I'll just go down there and get it. I have the other key at the bank. I'll be risking my job if I get caught, but I'm about to quit anyway. I got another offer to be a Branch Manager at one of their competitors. Plus, it sounds like fun." She smiled at him and they moved toward the cash register.

"This may not be as much fun as you think, especially if you get caught."

She shrugged her shoulders and placed her container on the conveyor belt while grabbing a Diet Coke from the mini fridge. Seth snagged a Coke for himself and put his container behind hers. "I got both," he said to the cashier, a freckled face woman in her late thirties. Madison thanked him for the gesture.

The cashier bagged both salads separately and Seth paid with his debit card. He grabbed the receipt and they headed for the door.

"Wait," Seth said. He grabbed her arm and pulled her against the wall. "I don't want them seeing us together. Are you sure about this?"

"Yeah, why not? Listen, I'll try to get it today and

I'll bring it home with me. You and your granddad can come over my house tonight and look through it."

"I don't like this at all," he said.

"What other choice do you have? I'll be fine."

"Okay, but be careful." He reached into his pocket and took out the key that he convinced his granddad should stay with him.

She smiled, took the key and gave him her address, which he plugged into his phone's notepad and they exchanged phone numbers. She said, "See you tonight," and left the store.

Seth waited almost five minutes before he exited with his lunch and then went back to his car and ate it inside. He thought about the past seventy-two hours. Friday night, Granddad's house, found key. Saturday at the yard sale, creepy bald guy. Saturday night, met Madison, the only bright spot. Sunday, saw Granddad, another bright spot in a way. Monday, followed to the diner, to Harper's Grove, to the bank, found some book inside a safety deposit box that hasn't been opened in twenty-five years. Searched and threatened by two men. Just your typical weekend.

His granddad didn't expect him when he arrived a few hours later at Harper's Grove. He told the receptionist on duty that he was taking Arthur to a movie. She said that was okay as long as he was back at Harper's Grove by eight o'clock sharp. She even said the word 'sharp'. They got into the car in silence and Seth explained the plan that Madison laid out.

"Brilliant!" exclaimed Arthur. "I knew she was a keeper."

"Granddad, she could get in trouble," Seth replied.

Arthur put his calloused, wrinkled hands on the dashboard and drummed along to whatever nineties hit was on the car radio.

"I feel alive, Seth! For the first time since I got to this god-forsaken place, I have something to do, some kind of purpose."

Seth pulled over to the side of the parking lot and shut off the car.

"What? Let's go!" Arthur exclaimed.

"Not before you tell me what's going on and what's in the book," Seth responded. He had to admit, this was the most energy his grandfather exhibited in a long time. He was glad, but he also worried about the danger that might lie ahead.

Arthur undid his seatbelt, opened the door and said, "Get out." He walked to the side of the parking lot where there was grass and even a small pond stocked with Koi fish. He put his foot up on the rocks that surrounded the pond and stared down into the water before reaching into his pocket and pulling out a pack of cigarettes. "Stole these from Miss Cartwright." He paused and playfully put the cigarette in and out of his mouth. "Back when I was your age, what are you twenty-five?"

"I'm thirty-two, Granddad."

"Right, well years ago, this had to be when I was about twenty, we're talking 1960, I had a conversation with a man who told me about this book."

"Yeah, but what's in it?"

Arthur shrugged his shoulders. "Beats me. There's not much in it, most of it is maps and drawings. Some are cryptic, some are not. I tried to figure it out when I was your age, as I'm sure this man's ancestors did before us. I tried to crack that riddle for years but then I gave up on it and put it away for safe keeping."

"Whose book is it?"

Arthur smiled. "You'll see."

"And you have no idea what it's about?" asked Seth.

"I have no idea, boy. But I'll tell you one thing…"

"What?"

"Me and you are going to read that book frontways and backways. We're gonna solve that puzzle. Maybe even get that girly of yours to help."

Seth looked at the old man and knew he should've objected but he just couldn't. He hadn't seen his granddad this happy and full of spunk in a while. Somehow, he had to keep his father from knowing that he was taking his dad on a wild goose chase. Seth walked to him and put his arm around his shoulder, leading him back to the car. "Let's go find out what's in that book."

CHAPTER 7

Seth received a text message on his way to Madison's house that she indeed had gotten into the safety deposit box and retrieved the book. He picked up a pizza and Arthur made him stop at the liquor store for a bottle of scotch, single-malt, imported, from anywhere but Scotland. He parked the car, grabbed the pizza and walked up to Madison's house. She opened the door and they went in.

"A drink first!" exclaimed Arthur.

Madison gave Seth a sidelong glance and he shrugged his shoulders. Seth took in the surroundings of the small ranch house. Small was the first thought that came to his mind. Granted, she had a house and he didn't. It was sparsely furnished with a TV and a couch and a soft velvety brown recliner in the living room. No coffee table, no end tables, no futon, no TV stand. They followed Arthur into the kitchen where he busied himself opening and closing cabinets.

"Where's a glass, dear?" Arthur asked.

Madison walked over to the far counter and reached into a cabinet and pulled out a small glass. Arthur took it and the bottle of scotch and settled into a chair at the kitchen table.

"Now, where's that book?"

They both looked at him for a brief moment before Madison left the room.

"Sorry, where are my manners. Can I pour you one?" he asked Seth as he twisted the cap off the green bottle and splashed more than three fingers of the malt into his glass.

"No, thanks," replied Seth.

"I have beer in the fridge, Seth," Madison called from the hallway.

Arthur brought the small glass to his lips, sniffed the rusty liquid, swirled the contents around in a circle, toasted to an imaginary drinking buddy, and took a long swallow.

"Ahh," Arthur said, staring at the glass. "Can't remember the last time I've had a drink." He reached into the pizza box and grabbed a slice of the sausage and mushroom pie.

Seth opened the fridge, grabbed two Sierra Nevada's and started opening drawers, looking for a bottle opener. Madison walked in and placed the book on the table away from Arthur.

"You're not touching this book until you finish eating. Look how fragile these pages are. I have no idea what it even is, but I know it doesn't deserve your grease-stained hands on it."

Arthur put on a fake smile and continued eating his

pizza. Madison found the opener and used it to open the two beers. She grabbed some paper plates and brought everything over to the kitchen table.

"I'm not eating until we look at this book," she said.

"I agree," Seth said and picked up the small leather book. He opened it to the first page and Madison and Arthur leaned in close.

Inscribed on the first page were the initials "G" and "W" and "February 22, 1732".

"GW? What's that?" asked Seth.

"Only the most famous GW that ever lived," replied Arthur.

It took only about ten seconds before Madison asked, "George Washington?"

"Really? Wow," was all Seth could manage to say.

"You mean we're holding a book that was written by George Washington?" Madison asked.

"Holy crap," Seth responded.

Arthur nodded his head and said, "Keep reading."

He turned to the next page and saw a paragraph of words. The script was black, long and fluid, and the words almost ran into each other. Seth squinted and started to read aloud. "It was. No…that's not right. It is? I can't make any of this out."

"Here, let me read it," Arthur said. "I've already seen it before." He turned the book toward him and began.

It is with great displeasure that I am writing this. My days are coming to an end and I can no longer keep this to myself. Let me tell you that I did what I did under great duress and for the betterment of the country. I will not reveal anything here in this journal. But, if you are worthy enough, it will reveal itself. The revelation could change the future of this great land, so use this knowledge only for the betterment of these states which we now call America. Respectfully, G Washington.

"What's he talking about, Granddad?" Seth asked.

"That's what we need to figure out, son."

They re-read the cryptic message in silence.

"But how?" Madison asked.

"Inside," Arthur flipped a few pages, "are some signs and clues that tell us either where something is, or the actual something itself. I couldn't figure anything out twenty-five years ago but I didn't try hard enough." He turned a page and said, "Look here. This is a list of the Washington family."

John Washington

Augustine Washington ~ Mary Washington

Lawrence ~ Augustine ~ George

Martha

John ~ Martha ~ Eleanor ~ George

BUSHROD

"Bushrud? What kind of name was that?" Seth asked.

"It's Bushrod," Arthur answered, emphasizing the *rod*. "I remember some of these people. I did some research in the library back then. Bushrod was his nephew."

"Why's it in capital letters?" Madison asked.

"Don't know. John and Martha were his kids from Martha's previous marriage, and Eleanor and George were his grandkids."

"Really?" Seth asked.

Arthur just shrugged his shoulders.

Madison left the room and came back with her laptop. She powered it up and Googled George Washington. While searching, she grabbed a slice of pizza. Seth did the same and Arthur poured himself another drink. After a few moments she found what she needed and read aloud. "Yep, Bushrod was his nephew and the other four were Martha's and his grandkids. Says here that Washington was rumored to have been sterile. Something about an earlier battle with smallpox. That date on the first page? That was the day he was born."

"There's gotta be something about Bushrod," Seth said. "He doesn't have any other cousins, uncles or nephews listed. Also, the name is in capital letters. What's it say about him?"

"I'm looking, I'm looking....here." She read quietly to herself. "Nothing, really. It just says that George always had a special relationship with his nephew. Maybe because he was blood related, unlike his children who he adopted as his own."

"Anyway, back to the diary," Arthur said, turning the page. Madison took another bite of pizza and walked back to lean over Arthur's shoulder.

"These next pages stopped me cold," said Arthur. They stared down at a sketch of some sort. It looked like a child's connect the dots activity page. There was a sequence of letters starting with A and ending with E that were sprinkled sporadically on the page. "I copied the image onto a piece of paper and connected the dots. Looked like stars to me so I compared them to all of the constellations in the sky. Nothing ever fit."

They stared silently at the page, the only sound coming from the clinking of ice in Arthur's glass.

"I haven't a clue either," Seth replied. "Madison, gimme a piece of paper."

She went over to the island in the kitchen and opened a drawer and came out with a notepad and a pencil. She crouched next to Arthur and tried to copy the image as it was shown on the page. After a few seconds, she had the image drawn and had connected the dots, A through E.

Seth leaned over. "Okay, let's come back to that, what else is in the book?"

A knock sounded at the front door. And not a subtle tap-tap—a fist pound, with knuckles. All three of them froze, Madison with her mouth open, Seth's around a bite of sausage, and Arthur in mid-swallow of booze.

Seth was the first to speak. "You expecting anyone?"

Madison shook her head. "Think it's those guys you were talking about?"

Seth got up from his chair, went over to the window, and moved the drapes out of the way. "Yep, black SUV. Shit!"

Arthur closed the book and grabbed the sketch they had just drawn. He paced around the kitchen muttering something to himself.

Pound-Pound-Pound

"Now what?" she asked.

"Gotta open it sometime," Seth replied. "They see my car so they know I'm in here. Want me to get it?"

She walked toward the door and said, "No, it's my house. They can't just barge in here. Arthur, hide that book!"

Arthur looked around and tossed it in the only thing he could think of: the microwave. Seth gave him a disapproving look and sat down on the couch in the living room while Madison put one hand on the deadbolt and the other on the doorknob. She shrugged her shoulders and opened the door. Standing outside was a heavy-set man chewing gum. He spoke first while his eyes scanned Madison up and down.

"I was hoping it was you who opened the door," he said.

"Can I help you?" she asked, clearly annoyed.

"I'm sure you can, but right now, I need to talk to your boyfriend and the old man."

"Sorry, they can't be bothered." Madison started to close the door but the man stuck his foot out and blocked it from closing.

He leaned in close to her and said, "Listen sweetheart, you tell that boy to get out here and talk to me right now or we can make your life a lot more difficult." He sniffed the air like a dog and waited for her response.

"You repulse me, wait here."

Madison left the door open a crack and turned around and almost bumped into Seth.

"I'll handle it," Seth said.

"I'll be watching from the window, and I'm calling 9-1-1 if anything happens."

Seth stepped outside and walked the few steps down the path to the man leaning against the SUV. The air was crisp and cool, and a light breeze rattled the leaves in the trees. By the time he had gotten there, the bald guy was out of the car, waiting. The other guy lit up a cigarette when Seth approached.

This time, Seth spoke first. "At least tell me your names so I don't refer to you as the bald guy and the heavy guy."

"Sure, let's make this as peaceful as possible," said Kohler. "I'm Abbott and this is Costello. That suit you?"

"Perfect. Now, what the hell do you guys want?"

"You know what the hell we want," replied Costello, otherwise known as Pierce.

Kohler turned to his partner and with a glance, basically told him to shut his mouth.

"Seth," Abbott started, "just give us whatever you found in that bank vault and we'll be out of your hair."

"We didn't find anything."

"See, that's a lie. Know how I can tell?" Abbott started pacing around Seth in circles. "And no, you didn't glance left like you hear in the movies when someone lies. You denied it Seth."

"What am I supposed to say when I don't have it?"

"No, you denied it too quickly. A normal person who didn't have anything would ask what it was. You didn't. Why? Because you already know what it is. Me? I don't know and I don't care. I have a job to do."

"For who?" Seth asked.

"None of your damn business," replied Costello, stamping his cigarette in the ground.

"As my fine partner just said, it's none of your business. Listen Seth, if you don't hand over what you found, I'll destroy your apartment with sledgehammers, and the old man's house, and your pretty girlfriend's house too. Or," he stopped pacing and leaned in close to him, "Maybe I'll put a couple of kilos of coke in your house and get a search warrant to look through it."

That caught Seth off guard. "A warrant? What are you, cops?"

Abbott looked back at his partner and they both chuckled a little bit. Abbott leaned in closer to Seth and turned toward his right ear and whispered, "If you were only so lucky." He brushed an imaginary hair off his jacket and opened the door to the SUV. His partner went around the other side and got into the driver's seat. The car started and Abbott rolled down his window as Seth was about to walk back up to the house.

"Twenty-four hours, Seth. Eight PM tomorrow night. And don't try to call the cops, the National Guard, nobody. Just you, with the package, outside the front steps of this house."

CHAPTER 8

Jonathon Castle received the report from his team in the field, Abbott and Costello, real names, Kohler and Pierce, that the kid was still denying that he had found anything of value. According to his guys, they followed him back and forth the past few days, from the retirement home, to his apartment, to the bank, and now to the girl's house. Castle had a dilemma to ponder. He could either swoop in now and grab the book with force and possibly cause a firestorm, or he could let the kid uncover what the book contained and then take the real treasure for himself.

Castle paced in his study which was lined from floor to ceiling on one side with windows and on the other side, framed photographs of famous golf holes around the world. He removed his red striped tie and threw it over the leather chair behind his desk. Castle was a big man, almost six feet two and weighing in at close to two hundred and fifty pounds. He had been trim in his days at Yale while on the crew team, but he no longer had the time or the energy to do much physical activity. The last twenty or thirty pounds seemed to creep up on him these past few years as he approached sixty. His hair started to gray around thirty, and since then he'd kept it close to the scalp, a buzz cut.

It was nearing midnight on the east coast. He pondered whether to make an important phone call and then opened the bottom drawer of his large desk made of oak, lifted up a few manila folders, and found his nectar, Jim Beam Black. He was never a bourbon or whiskey kind of guy, and always preferred clear spirits like gin and vodka. The problem was they weren't good straight. He needed some tonic, or club, splash of lime or some fruit juice, so he switched over to bourbon. This way he could hide the small bottle in his office and take a swig whenever the need occurred, which was right now.

He twisted the cap and tilted the small bottle to his lips. The liquor didn't settle on his tongue long before it flooded down his esophagus and entered his blood stream, warming him immediately. He wiped his hand across his mouth and took another smaller drink before putting the bottle back in the drawer, tucking it away neatly in the back.

Castle scrolled through his private cell phone, found the number he needed and sat down at his desk. He had only called this man once, and that was after the man called him a few months ago. Other than that, they exchanged email with each other a few times. Castle wasn't sure why he wanted to call him right now. Reassurance? Motivation? Help? He punched the green button on his phone and dialed the number.

After several rings someone picked up. “Bannister.”

Castle cleared his throat before responding, “Hey, it’s me, Jon Castle.”

“Jon? What the hell you calling me at this hour for?”

“It’s just, we got a lead.”

“You haven’t found it yet?”

“Well, we think we have located it, yes. It’s not in my possession yet, but it will be soon. I may even let the kid find it for me.”

“You’ll do no such thing, Jon. Find it yourself. I found out what I need to know, now you go and get the proof. You hearin’ me? We don’t need this kid finding it that’s for sure.” Bannister could be heard on the other end of the line breathing very hard.

“You alright?” Castle asked.

“On the treadmill,” Bannister replied, the words broken up by deep breaths.

“At this hour?”

“Only time I can squeeze it in. Now Jon, what are your men saying?”

“They said they think the kid’s got it but they’re not sure.”

“Not sure? They either have it or they don’t. Have you told your men that it’s a book?”

“Not exactly, just something old and valuable. I kinda hinted it may be a book.”

“What the bloody hell, Jon. Hold on.” In the background of the phone, you could hear a few electronic beeps. Then, what appeared to be Bannister swallowing a large amount of liquid. He came back on the line, his breathing more controlled. "What's the address of this kid?"

"Huh? Why?"

"Jon, don't make me fly across the Atlantic and beat the bloody piss out of you. Give me the address."

Castle gave him the address of both the kid and the girl and a few moments later they hung up. The last words he heard were, "If you want something done right, you gotta do it yourself," followed by a few expletives. He opened the drawer once more and fished for the bottle in the back, his last indulgence of the night.

Seth came back inside and informed Arthur and Madison of the predicament they were currently in. He told them about the threat of a warrant and they all pondered for a few moments who the men were and who hired them. They spoke about the twenty-four hour deadline before they had to turn over the book.

"Wait a second," Seth said. They were once again seated around the kitchen table, eating the pizza. "They never even mentioned what kind of book. They said something about a 'package', and 'whatever you found'. They don't know what we have in our hands. We just give them some other book that looks old and worn tomorrow night."

"That won't work in the long run," Madison stated, "but it will at least buy us some more time with this thing. Whoever wants it will find it, and who knows what they will do to get it."

Seth took small sips of his beer and nibbled at his pizza. Arthur and Madison paged through the book until finally Madison broke the silence. "What?" she asked while looking up at Seth.

He shook his head and curled his lower lip over his upper lip as if to say, "nothing."

"Seth, what are you thinking about, son?" Arthur asked.

Seth did not raise his eyes up from his bottle of beer that he was slowly pulling the label from when he spoke. "It's weird, you know. Why do we care about this book? Why not give it back to them?"

Madison raised her voice. "What?" Arthur reached over and put his hand on her arm but she shook free. "You basically had me commit a felony today for which I could not only get fired but possibly face jail time and now you wanna quit on this?"

"I'm just saying we don't even know what it is and we're getting threatened and followed to the point that I don't know if it's worth continuing."

"Seth," Arthur jumped in, "this book, whatever it is, has been in my hands for quite some time now. I feel it's my duty to find out what's in it. Added to which, if this book was not that important, we *wouldn't* be followed and threatened. What kind of legitimate business or establishment goes to all this trouble if it was all on the up and up?"

Now it was Madison's turn. "He's right, Seth. That's the million dollar question. Not what's in the book, but rather, who needs to know what's in the book so badly that they would go to all the trouble of following us and threatening us?"

Arthur got up from his seat with his glass of rusty-colored liquid, walked over to Seth on the other side of the table and put his hand on his shoulder. "Son, this is the most excitement this old man has had in years. I'm in it for the long haul and I want you with me."

Madison grabbed her beer and tilted it to the both of them, "I'm in," she said.

Seth looked up at his granddad and said, "If anything happens to you, Dad will kill me."

Arthur smiled. "Don't worry about him, I can still whoop his ass."

Seth raised his beer, "I'm in." They all said "cheers" and took a nice long pull of their drinks. "Now, what else is in that book?"

Madison and Arthur returned to their seats on the other side of the table and Seth went to the fridge to grab two more beers. If nothing else, he was certainly enjoying Madison's company and would extend the night as long as possible to be near her.

"Well," Madison started, "there's not much more here. The page after the A through E drawing is just a picture of the American Flag. See?" She turned the book to Seth and it showed the original American Flag. Thirteen dots, stars, if drawn to scale, in a circle in the upper left hand corner, thirteen stripes covering the rest of the flag.

"After that is another connect the dot page, F through K," Madison said while getting another piece of paper and tracing the dots. They compared both pages and could not make heads or tails around what the drawing was supposed to depict.

"What if you continued the line from E to F on the paper so it flows together?" Seth asked. Madison connected both pages and they still had nothing. The A-E drawing was larger than the F through K and they tried endless combinations to conjoin the two. A on the left, A on the right, on the bottom, on the top, even upside down.

"What about under it?" Seth asked.

"What do you mean?" Madison replied.

"Here," Seth said while grabbing the two sheets of paper. He put the F-K sheet on top of the A-E sheet and stared at the new image. "Can't see much."

"Put it under the light," Arthur said.

Seth put it directly under the kitchen light and now they could make out the dots on the page underneath. They formed a picture of sorts. Seth added in the dots from the page beneath to the page on top and they now had a full pictogram from A through K.

"Got it," said Seth.

Madison did too and after just a moment, they both said the words together, "A house."

Arthur took a sip of his drink and wiped his mouth with the back of his hand. "All these years of guessing and all I had to do was put one page under the other. Why the hell would he do that?"

"Cause it's a game, Granddad. He wants us to find something or discover something, but then again he doesn't, so he makes it difficult."

The house they created by connecting the letters was small and narrow in size. There were no windows or doors drawn out, but you could tell it was three stories high with a chimney on the left hand side.

"Nice job Seth." Madison walked over to Seth and clinked his beer bottle with hers. For a brief moment, they locked eyes and she smiled before taking a swig of her beer. "Now, we're getting somewhere."

"So, we're looking for a flag in a house. Maybe we're looking for a flag on top of a house?" Seth asked.

"Who puts a flag on top of a house?" Arthur asked. "Maybe a building, firehouse, or on a flagpole, but not on top of a house."

"Granddad, if this book or diary is authentic, which we kind of believe, it was written in the seventeen hundreds. We have to think like that, not like the world we live in today."

"That's true Seth," Madison said, "but what house is still in existence today that was built in the seventeen hundreds?"

"The White House?" Seth replied.

"Nope," Arthur replied. "Washington D.C. wasn't even the capital back then, so George Washington could not have described that. D.C. became the capital in 1800. You know what the capital was, don't you? That's right, good old Philadelphia. Washington spent a lot of time in this area. That house we're looking for could be right under our noses."

"So we have to search every house in the city that was built in the seventeen hundreds and still exists today?" Seth asked.

"And still has a flag on it," Madison chimed in.

"Yeah, that'll be fun, gosh." Seth said sarcastically. "What else is in the book?"

The three of them leaned in close to the book on the table. Arthur turned the next page and on it was another "connect the dots" sort of pictogram. It was true, Madison discovered on the internet, George Washington often drew plots of land or maps with a pictogram. He would walk acres and acres of land while plotting points on a piece of canvas. Then, he would connect the dots to form an accurate portrayal of the land. The one they were looking at now was more simplistic. There were seven dots on the left and seven dots on the right, all equally proportionate. In between the sixth row, there were five dots gathered close together. Seth took the liberty of recreating the drawing on a piece of paper. All he had come up with was a series of lines that ran horizontal to each other, like cornrows. In the middle of the sixth however, a shape came to life.

"A star," Madison guessed first.

"Looks that way to me," Seth responded.

"Which means what?"

"That's what we have to figure out," Arthur said.

"So after we find the flag place we look for this shape? Maybe the star is like the 'X' that marks the spot."

"A treasure?" Arthur said, perking up.

"I don't think it's a treasure, Granddad. Remember what he wrote in the front." Seth flipped back a few pages and read aloud. "'It is with great displeasure that I am writing this.' Whatever it is, he's ashamed of it."

"Damn, I wanna get rich. What else is in there, I forget? It has been twenty-five years since I read through it."

Seth flipped to the page after the last drawing and read: *Once you have found this location, you will have the necessary tools to find the great truth that must one day reveal itself. Do so with caution. Signed, G Washington.*

"What else?" Madison asked.

Seth flipped through but found nothing else written. "That's it."

"That's it? After two-hundred years of hiding, that's all we have to go on is two silly drawings?"

"Apparently so, let's get crackin'."

"Oh, look who's the enthusiastic one now, Arthur?" Both Madison and Arthur eyed Seth cautiously.

"Hey, this was your idea, I'm just playin' along."

"Right," Madison replied. "You wanna find whatever this is just as badly as we do."

Seth took a swallow of beer, shrugged his shoulders, smiled at her and said, "True."

Madison grabbed her laptop off the counter and brought it over to the table. Arthur headed off to the bathroom, so Seth moved in to the seat nearest her. They scoured various historic websites but mainly focused on Philadelphia's City Hall and the Independence Hall, home of the First Constitutional Convention. Both of the buildings were hundreds of years of old, but neither looked like the picture in the journal.

"Where's Arthur?" Madison suddenly asked.

Alarmed, and not noticing that he had not come back from the bathroom fifteen minutes before, he walked out into the living room and founded him asleep in the recliner. "Shit, I was supposed to get him back to his place tonight."

"At this hour? They've probably locked up and

won't care anyway. Just let him sleep here. We can take him back in the morning."

Seth perked up at that last comment. "We?" he asked.

Madison didn't miss a beat. "Yes, Seth, we. That means you and I. Both of us. He's sleeping here and you're sleeping here. I'm not staying here alone with those crazy guys out there."

Seth walked over to her and set his beer on the counter. "Is that the only reason you want me to stay here?"

Madison put her beer down next to his and grabbed both his hands in hers. She leaned in and kissed him hard on the lips, taking full control of the situation. After several moments she pulled away and ran her tongue along her upper lip. "Yes, that's the only reason. You get the couch.....at least for tonight."

Seth watched her turn the kitchen light out and head into her bedroom, closing the door behind her. "Damn," he muttered under his breath.

CHAPTER 9

The orange glow of the sun coming over the Atlantic in the east never left the tiny oval window inside the small plane. The man sitting in the window seat raised and lowered the plastic shade several times during the past two hours of his eight hour Trans-Atlantic flight. It was odd to take a red-eye flight across the Atlantic east to west, but several provisions had been made for the three person team. As the wheels touched down in Philadelphia, Maximus Church yawned once and looked over at his companions. The woman and the man were asleep almost as soon as the Gulfstream had taken off and were much more rested than he. He closed the Ian Rankin detective novel he was reading and unbuckled his seatbelt.

"Let's go, chaps, you slept enough," he said. When Max stood up, the white button-downed shirt he wore stretched across his tight muscles and he bent over at the knees to get the blood flowing in his legs. He walked down the aisle to the front of the plane, grabbed his matching gray sport coat and threw it over his arm. His tall frame and dark eyes turned and glanced back down toward the sleeping couple sitting across from him. He shook his head and walked toward them.

He approached the woman, put his hands on his hips and stared at the red-haired beauty. Chloe Tolliver was blessed in that all of her excess weight was distributed perfectly to her chest and her rear end. Barely cresting five feet, she still had measurements that made heads turn. What set her apart was her ability to separate her femininity from the job at hand. A smile came across his face and he grabbed her arm and placed her hand on the crotch of the man sitting next to her. An idea popped into his head and he pulled out his camera phone and snapped a quick picture. He stepped back and chuckled to himself.

SMACK!

Max clapped his hands together not ten inches from her face. The man next to her was the first to open his eyes. Evan Long raised his head and took in his surroundings. It took him about five seconds to feel his partner's hand covering his masculinity. Before Evan could even get aroused, Chloe woke and took much less than five seconds to evaluate the situation.

She removed her hand from Evan's crotch and exclaimed, "What the hell?"

Max couldn't help but laugh at the two of them. Chloe blushed and straightened her gray jacket and stared off in the distance.

"You two fuckers have fun on the flight?" Max asked.

"Shut the hell up, Max," Chloe replied. "Stop messin' around, Evan."

"Bullshit! I slept the whole time," Evan said. "You must've been dreaming about me, eh Chloe?"

"In *your* dreams, Evan." She crossed her arms and looked out the window as the small plane taxied toward the gate.

"Don't worry," Max said, waving the phone in front of them, "I won't show *everyone*."

Chloe unbuckled her seatbelt and lunged for the phone, but Max was too quick and too tall. He held it high above her head.

"Settle down and let's get the bloody hell outta here."

Max was still holding the phone too high for Chloe's grasp. She sighed and gathered her belongings in the seat next to her and the overhead compartment: a small navy backpack and a small rolling suitcase that she always traveled with. No purse, she didn't need one. Born with natural beauty, she rarely wore makeup unless she was working undercover.

The plane came to a stop near a small hangar on the outskirts of Philadelphia International Airport. The door opened and out dropped a short staircase to the tarmac below. The three of them made their way down the stairs and were greeted by a man who wore cargo shorts, a blue logo golf shirt, orange vest and large earphones. He didn't bother to raise his thick sunglasses as he spoke.

"Maximus Church?"

"Right here," Max said, raising his arm.

"These are for you," the man said, pointing to a

small, motorized vehicle behind him. On the back of the flatbed was a large six foot long piece of black and silver luggage, appearing to be what golfers used to fly with their bag and clubs.

"Thanks," Max said walking over and hoisting the hard plastic case off the bed of the truck. He flipped open the latches and looked inside. It was just as he expected, a golf bag with golf clubs.

Evan came over and peered inside as well. "What's up mate? You golfin' in the states, mate?" except it sounded a lot more like 'goffing'.

"No, dipshit," Max replied. He unzipped the long side pocket and looked inside. Three handguns, nine ammunition clips and three sets of handcuffs were inside. "We're definitely not golfing."

The phone on the table rattled and spun as the vibrations took hold of the small device every two point three seconds. After the sixth vibration, Seth was conscious enough to open his eyes and take in his surroundings. He was on the couch in Madison's house. He looked to his left and saw his granddad snoring away on the recliner. Seth reached for the phone on the coffee table but missed the caller. He checked the missed call and saw that it was his dad calling. Another twenty seconds later, his phone vibrated again indicating a message. He looked at the time displayed on his phone. It was just before seven in the morning. Seth tossed it back on the table, rubbed his eyes and got up from the couch.

After relieving himself in the hall bathroom, he

went to the kitchen and fuddled through the cabinets searching for coffee. "Nice," he said as he found the opened pound of Starbucks coffee and filters to go with it. Within minutes the coffee was brewing. He checked his phone for email and messages as he waited. The voicemail was from his dad who wanted him to call him back.

"Mornin'," Madison said, appearing from around the corner of the living room. Half of her was hidden behind the corner, but the white tank top on and long pink pajama pants she wore enticed him.

"Hey," was all he could manage to say.

"Thanks for making coffee. Nice waking up to that smell. Thanks for staying here."

"No biggie. Thanks for letting that guy sleep here too," he replied, thumbing toward his granddad on the recliner.

She walked into the kitchen, opened the cabinet, pulled three coffee mugs out and arranged them on the counter. Seth opened the fridge, grabbed the milk and proceeded to doctor his own mug. Madison carried her cup out of the kitchen and said over her shoulder, "I'm gonna go shower."

Seth watched her from behind, staring long after she disappeared around the corner. In his search for milk he spotted some fixings in the refrigerator for a good breakfast. In no time, he'd made a green pepper omelet and topped it with melted cheese and salsa. He separated it onto three plates and laid them on the kitchen table. He went into the living room and stirred his granddad awake, pulled out his cell phone and returned the call to his father.

"Hey Dad, what's up?"

"Hey son, how's it goin' up there?"

Seth looked at his granddad while he stumbled into the kitchen to pour himself a cup of coffee, black. He held up one finger to his lips knowing there was no way he could tell his dad that he snuck his own father out of his home and kept him overnight.

"Nothing much. Why what's up?"

There was a long pause before his father spoke. "Seth, your granddad's doctor called, and he needs a new liver. Quick," he added.

Seth looked over at his granddad shoveling the omelet into his mouth and giving him a thumbs up as if to say, *good breakfast*. "What's *quick* mean?"

"Six weeks," his dad blurted out.

"Jeez." Out of the corner of his eye he noticed his granddad looking at him. "Well, okay," his voice grew louder, "that sounds good, I'll call you later."

"Wait, Seth—"

Seth ended the call and sat down at the table with his granddad. His phone vibrated again in his pocket. It was his dad; he ignored the call.

"Who was that?" his granddad asked.

"Ah, just work."

Madison strolled into the kitchen. "Mmm, Mexican for breakfast?"

"I can eat Mexican food anytime," Seth responded.

"Me too." She sat down at the table and joined them. Her hair was still wet, and the curls clung to her neck. She wore a green tank top with sparkles around the neck and snug fitting dark jeans. As she sat, she tucked her right leg under her left and bounced it up and down. She looked over at Seth who watched her intently. She took a bite of the omelet and winked with her left eye. "Good work," she said.

"Now, what's the plan today?" Arthur asked, finishing his omelet in record time and wiping his mouth with a napkin.

"We start with finding that building with the flag on it," Seth said.

"Then let's go," Arthur replied, "no time to waste."

Both Seth and Madison finished their breakfast and coffee and cleared the table. As they packed up, ready to leave, Arthur came back into the kitchen. "We have a slight problem, those guys are back and waiting outside."

They all went into the living room and pulled back enough of the curtains to see the SUV across the street and the two guys from last night sitting inside.

"Shit," Seth said. "They're going to follow us all day."

"Maybe not," Madison said. "I'm going out the front into my car. You two go out the back, through the gate in the backyard and through the neighbor's yard behind mine. You'll be on the other block in thirty seconds."

"Okay, but they'll still follow you."

"No they won't. Your car is still out front, they'll think you're still inside. They only have one car so they'll stay here and wait for you to come out, which you won't."

With that the plan was hatched and executed. Abbott and Costello were a little confused when they only saw Madison come out of the house and hop in her car. Reluctantly, they stayed and waited for Seth and Arthur to come out but they never did. Madison picked them up around the block and they headed toward Center City Philadelphia.

Seth called Harper's Grove and told them he was taking his grandfather out for the day. He pulled the laptop out and was reading online about the various buildings in the city as she drove. "Well, scratch out City Hall. That building was built in 1871, way after Washington's time."

"At least that narrows our search," Madison said.

"Then head to Independence Hall," Seth replied, typing away.

"I don't know the address either, somewhere around Sixth and Walnut, I think."

"You two have never been to Independence Hall?" Arthur asked. "Never seen the Liberty Bell? You should be ashamed of yourselves, living in this town so long."

"I have, back in grade school. But that's it," Seth replied.

"Same here," Madison chimed in.

Arthur just shook his head from the backseat. "It's Sixth and Chestnut."

The Audi exited Interstate 95 and proceeded onto Route 676 toward Philadelphia. It was only a couple of blocks before they found the huge city block with grass and concrete pathways. Madison turned the car into an underground garage where they parked. They walked out into the sunlight, found their bearings and headed for the signs pointing the way toward Independence Hall.

The three of them took their time, taking in all of the sites and attractions that surrounded the park. The first statue they saw was of John Barry. It was tall, almost twenty feet high. His arm was outstretched like he was leading the troops into battle. Arthur stopped and read the inscription below that indicated his birth in 1745 and his death in 1803. Dubbed the 'Father of the American Navy', he and his crew fought and won the final naval battle of the American Revolutionary War.

In front of them now loomed Independence Hall. In the center, a four story building rose and was topped by a clock tower that stood another two stories high. It was attached to two-story buildings on either side. The building was constructed of red brick except the clock tower which was made of a pale gray stone.

"Wait a minute," Seth said. He stopped walking and pulled out the drawing from last night. "This is not it."

"No?" Madison asked.

"Look at the drawing we made." He leaned in close to her and together they glanced at the drawing, then back to the building, then down again. "The building we're looking for is very small. This place is huge." He pointed toward the building.

"What about those side buildings?" she asked.

Seth glanced down at the drawing once more. "I still don't see it. The place we're looking for is two stories with an attic or a small third story." He looked down again. "And a chimney!"

Madison could sense he was right. The place on the paper looked like a stand-alone building, not some huge place like Independence Hall.

Seth looked around the park. "Where's my granddad?"

"He was here a second ago."

"Shit, come on, he couldn't have gotten far."

They walked behind the statue and through a small open gate that led them closer to the Hall. When they approached the entrance, they saw Arthur talking to a man dressed as Benjamin Franklin.

"Granddad," Seth began, "don't walk away from us like that."

"Son, you know the Liberty Bell used to be right up there in that tower? Ben here has some memory. Better than mine."

They all turned and looked up at the huge building and found the bell tower.

"Not kept there anymore," the faux actor said. "It's across the street now at the Liberty Bell Center. Same Bell though, two thousand pounds of her. Same crack, all twenty-four and a half inches."

"See, listen to that!" Arthur said.

Seth pulled the paper out of his pocket and was about to open his mouth before Madison grabbed his arm. She whispered, "Don't ask."

The two of them walked a few steps away and Seth was the first to speak. "Why not?"

"Why get him involved? If we're being watched right now, then so is he."

Seth looked around the complex park. Lots of people walked the pathways, others studied the statues, parents held their children's hands, older couples read maps. Anyone could be out there watching them.

"But he could help us," Seth pleaded.

"The less information he knows the better."

He looked down and realized she was still holding his arm. "You're right," he said. They walked back to Ben Franklin and told Arthur it was time to go.

"He says this here on our left is Old City Hall and on the right is Congress Hall," Arthur said, pointing.

"Cool, let's go Granddad, lots to see here today." He grabbed his arm and led him away from Ben Franklin.

"What's the big rush? I liked talking to him," Arthur said.

"This is not the place," Seth replied. "Time to move on."

"To where?" Arthur asked.

"I have no idea," replied Seth, "do you, Madison?"

She didn't respond at first. Her eyes were locked on something across the park.

"Madison?" Seth asked.

She kept her gaze in the distance and replied, "I know where we're going next."

"Huh? Where?"

Madison looked over at Seth and smiled. She then turned her head back to what she was looking at. Seth followed her eyes. He was looking at the buildings, but none of them fit the one they wanted.

"Look at the people, not the buildings," she said.

"The people?" Arthur asked.

Both men looked back in the same direction she was looking. There were kids running in the park, their parents trying to catch up. There was a man dressed as Uncle Sam handing out balloons. Then he saw it. Or rather, saw her.

"Damn!" Seth said.

Near the corner of the park was a chubby little woman with a bonnet on her head and small wire-rimmed glasses. Her hands were tucked inside her long flowing dress that covered her feet. A dress that depicted the American Flag.

"Betsy Ross," Seth said.

CHAPTER 10

The small apartment outside Philadelphia was trashed in less than thirty minutes. Maximus and his team from across the pond had found Seth's place of living with the address given to them from their boss. They arrived shortly before noon and tore the place apart. The three of them emptied drawers and closets, they searched everywhere for the missing book their boss told them was in Seth's possession. Chloe let Max and Evan do the physical labor while she was more selective in her search. She watched Max turn over mattresses and Evan flip over couches, while she checked Seth's calendar, his voicemail machine, and his desktop computer. But they found nothing.

Evan leaned up against the couch he had just turned over. "Now what?"

"Now we go to the old man's house is what," replied Max.

"It's not going to be in that house, we gotta find

that kid."

"Says who? That's where the boss says it's been for the past twenty years. It's probably still there."

"Bannister said the kid found it."

"He only thinks he found it," Max said back to him.

Chloe had enough. "Shut up you two. Let's think a minute. I don't want to call Bannister just yet without finding anything. I agree with Evan, it's not at the old man's house anymore." She sensed Max was going to protest and held up her hand. "That being said, our next bet is the girl's house. Where's she live?"

Max pulled out his phone and scrolled through a couple of applications until he found his notepad. He took the address and plugged it into the phone's GPS system. Seconds later he said, "Fifteen minutes from here."

"Okay, let's grab a bite to eat and head to her house. But," she held up her hand again, "I don't want to trash that house. I think if they found the book, which obviously we all think they have, it's not at her house. They have it on them."

"Then what?" Evan asked.

"We wait until they get home and beat the piss out of them until they give it up," Max chimed in.

The trip from Independence Hall to the Betsy Ross House was only a couple of blocks. They walked up to the faux Betsy herself and asked directions to her house. She told them to proceed down Arch Street then turn on 3rd and follow the signs. Arthur was trailing behind, clearly getting winded from all of the walking they did today. Seth offered to grab a taxi, but Arthur refused. As they got closer to their destination, Madison picked up her pace, but twenty yards from the house she slowed down. Seth stopped next to her and they both looked down at the drawing Seth was holding.

"This is it," he said.

"Sure is."

The Betsy Ross house looked almost identical to the drawing. It had the chimney on the left side and had a small window at the top of the house. It was very narrow and tall with two second floor windows and one on the first floor. The only difference was that the door was on the opposite side of where Washington had drawn it. Arthur caught up to them and asked, "That's it, isn't it?"

"Let's go inside," Seth said.

"Wait," Madison said, "What are we looking for?"

Seth reached into his pants pocket and pulled out the second drawing and said, "This," waving the paper at her. "It's gotta be some kind of bookshelf or something with levels almost like a stadium."

Arthur peered over his shoulder, "Or stairs," he said.

Madison raised her eyebrows and said, "Or stairs!"

"Let's go," Seth said.

Outside the house a few people were gathered, talking in groups of two or three. To the left side, they entered a small courtyard where people milled about. There was a snack bar, a few tables and chairs scattered about, and a middle-aged woman giving a lecture to a dozen children. They walked up to a ticket booth and asked to see a tour of the house.

"Three dollars for the self-tour, five dollars for the audio tour, please," the man at the counter said.

Seth pulled out his money clip and handed the man a ten dollar bill. "Three self-tours," he said.

"I want an audio tour," Arthur said.

Seth pulled out two more dollars and gave it to the man. "Two self-tours and one audio tour." The man took the money and reached behind him into a small box and handed Arthur a set of earphones and a small device about the size of a deck of cards. "Every time you enter a new room, push that button there."

Madison and Seth grabbed a brochure and they walked into the house. The first place they entered was a gift shop that sold various trinkets of Betsy Ross, the American Flag, or other things relating to Colonial Times. Through the shop, they came outside again and into a small open tunnel that led to a small room and a narrow winding staircase which climbed up.

They tried to examine the staircase but other tourists were behind them and they had little time to stop and search. On the next floor there was a small bedroom straight ahead and a bedroom on the left that held a few heirlooms such as glasses, a quill and notepad, and a snuff box. There was a set of stairs on the right that had a rope across them and a small sign that said "Closed". Madison made eye contact with Seth and she took her chance. She lifted her leg over the stairs and walked up to the next level.

Seth tried blocking the staircase with his body but he didn't have to do it long. Madison was back down in less than thirty seconds.

"Dead-end," she said.

"What about the steps?"

She shrugged her shoulders. "I don't see anything relevant."

They went back down the stairs, then down another staircase which took them to the basement. The ceilings were very low and it was eerily dark in the small narrow space. Other tourists were there looking at items on the wall, a musket in a glass case and a ladder that seemed to lead to a closed cellar door.

"There's nothing here," Seth said.

Arthur was busy listening intently to the audio tour and always pulling up the rear. They went back upstairs, through the kitchen and back out into the courtyard. Although the house was one of the most famous in Philadelphia, the tour had taken them less than ten minutes. Arthur handed back his headphones and transmitter to the man at the front door. Heads down, Seth and Madison led the way away from the house.

"Now what?" Seth asked.

"Well, we can't just go break in there and start ripping apart those steps," Madison replied.

"But if that's where we have to look, what else can we do?"

Arthur was standing there watching them discuss their newest quandary with a slight grin on his face. Madison noticed it first and said, "What?"

"Well, if cheapo over here," pointing his thumb at Seth, "had ponied up the extra two bucks for the audio tour, you would've heard exactly what I heard about those stairs."

"Which is?" Madison said impatiently, extending her arms.

"The stairs were completely eliminated from the house during the renovation of 1937. Some guy Kent offered up twenty-five grand to do the whole thing."

"That explains the front of the house changing," Seth said. "Did they say anything about moving the door to the other side of the house?"

"Yep," Arthur replied.

"So where are the stairs now?" Madison asked.

Arthur shrugged his shoulders. "Beats me," he said.

"Let's grab the laptop from the car and find out," Madison said.

"Whoa," Arthur said, holding out his hand to stop her. "I need some food before we go any further."

"Fine, Granddad, head on over to Eulogy Tavern, it's a few blocks from here on Chestnut. Madison and I will get the laptop and meet you there."

"Wait, you're not leaving him alone," Madison said.

"Well I'm not leaving you by yourself either," Seth replied.

"I can fend for myself," she replied.

"So can I," Arthur spoke up for himself.

Madison leaned in close and gave Seth a kiss on the lips. "I'll be there in ten minutes." Seth watched her walk away and turned back toward Arthur who was smiling.

"What?" he asked.

"Nothing," Arthur said. He turned down the street toward the tavern. "I like her."

Seth smiled and joined him. "So do I Granddad." They walked in silence for the first block as Seth thought about the news that his father told him earlier that morning. His granddad was dying and needed a new liver soon. Being with him these past few days he saw a renewed energy and spirit in him, something that Seth had not seen since his grandmother died a few years ago. As crazy as the thought sounded, he was having fun with the old guy.

"How've you been, Seth?"

Seth thought that was an odd question to ask at a time like this. "Fine, why?"

"Work going well?"

"Sure."

"Just wondering that's all," Arthur said.

Then it hit him. Seth hadn't spent this much time with his granddad in years. Many, many years. He used to spend summers at his grandparents beach house before he got to high school. Then girls came into the picture, then sports, then part-time jobs every summer, then college, then the real world. They saw each other on holidays, on birthdays and unfortunately at funerals. But that was for a couple of hours, not day after day. He felt guilty, especially with time running out. He started to say something but Arthur interrupted him.

"It's okay son. Everyone grows up now and again. Hell, I don't even see your father that much anymore. No need to explain why, I know why. But don't let that stop you from informing the old man about your life."

"I won't Granddad," Seth said. He felt like a child again as the words of his grandfather were spoken. He was close to tearing up but was interrupted by the swinging bell of someone walking out of Eulogy Tavern. Two young men in jeans and a t-shirt held the door as they walked in.

The place was dark, especially for lunchtime. There was a long bar on the left hand side and a few barstools on the right that bellied up to a wooden bar attached to a mirrored wall. Four or five people sat at the bar, none against the wall. Seth took in his surroundings, not expecting Abbott and Costello, but he wanted to be sure. They walked through the bar and found a table in the back.

A tall black-haired girl with a nose-ring dropped off their menus and said she'd be right back to take their order. Seth and Arthur each received two menus, one for beer and one for food. Eulogy was known for their extravagant Belgian beer selection. The menu showed they had twenty-one beers on tap and over three hundred in bottles.

"This is what I'm talking about," Arthur said.

"Why do you think I suggested going here?" Seth replied.

The girl came back, said her name was Marni and took their drink order, Seth explained they were waiting for one more person. "I'll have the Chimay," Seth said.

Arthur closed the menu. "Sure, why not?"

"You're not having too many," Seth said. "Hell, I don't even know why we're drinking, but a beer sounds good right now." He checked his watch and kept glancing at the door.

"Relax, son, she'll be fine."

Just then, the bell chimed and in walked Madison. "See?"

She poked her head above the other bar patrons and noticed them in the back. As she approached the table, she took the laptop out of the bag and laid it next to her. "So," she began, "you miss me?"

"Yep, now what do you want to drink?" Arthur responded. Marni came back and set the beers on the table. A huge creamy head of foam crested the pale yellow beer; Marni was careful not to spill a drop.

"Same as them," Madison told Marni.

"Are you guys ready to order?" she asked.

"Seth, order for all of us, why don't you?" Arthur responded, taking a sip of his beer. Madison chuckled as a gob of foam stuck to his nose.

Seth picked up the menu again and read aloud, "Okay, we'll have the fried calamari, the crispy crab, and the Belgian frittes."

"Wait a second, do you have burgers?" Arthur asked Marni. Before she could respond, he added, "I'll have a burger, medium, cheddar, bacon, mayonnaise, lettuce, and tomato. Thanks." He turned to Seth and said, "I can't eat that crap you ordered."

Madison opened up her laptop and powered it on. She typed while Seth sipped his beer and Arthur gulped his. She started her search and found the Kent that Arthur spoke about earlier.

"Okay, says here that Atwater Kent, a famous radio personality donated money to restore the house in 1937."

Arthur turned his palms over as if to say *told you*.

"A new structure was added in the rear, made from bricks. So that can't be our steps. The front doorway was moved and a new window was created. He then built a garden on either side of the house. That's it, nothing else."

"What did they do with the stairs or the old door?" Seth asked.

She scanned the rest of the page. "Doesn't say. Hold on, let me search his name." Marni brought Madison's beer and the frittes with bourbon re`moulade sauce. Frittes were the Belgian version of French fries only slightly darker, saltier, and crispier. Arthur's hand was the first to reach into the basket. "Atwater Kent was a radio pioneer and inventor in Philadelphia in the early nineteen hundreds. Hold on, here! In 1938, he built a museum in Philadelphia to celebrate the history of the city."

"Is it still around?" Seth asked.

Madison raised her glass of beer and took a long swallow. "The Atwater Kent Museum of Philadelphia is located on Seventh Street, just a few blocks from here."

Jon Castle had his daily briefings that morning but he couldn't concentrate. Up late to begin with, he was lucky the few drams of whiskey he had the night before knocked him out cold. As the last person finished talking, he reached into his pocket once more to check his cell phone. No messages. He got up from his leather chair at the head of the table and started to leave the conference room before his assistant, Kim Bevin, stopped him as he reached the door.

"Jon, what is it?" she asked. Kim had short dark hair, almost boyish, but it didn't take away from her good looks. Although a bit plump, she took to being a vegan the past six months and shed over half of the thirty pounds she needed to lose. This garnered notice from the opposite sex for the first time in her thirty-eight years, including Jon Castle. Kim put her hand on her boss' arm and looked him in the eye.

"Just tired, that's all," Jon responded. He looked away into the hallway and saw staffers bustling throughout the corridor.

Kim lowered her voice and leaned in closer to him. "You need to get some sleep and snap out of it, Jon. I know you've been distracted with something. If I'm starting to notice, I'm not the only one."

"It's nothing, really." In fact he was excited about the last few days up until he called his counterpart the night before. The realization that he was so close to what had eluded him for so long brought a euphoric sense of thrill. He was about to be *The Man*.

"Well it's something. Why don't you tell me?"

He thought for a few brief seconds and locked eyes with his young assistant. "Maybe there is something you can help me with. Block off two hours of my schedule around six o'clock and come by my office."

"Why not tell me now?"

He glanced out into the hallway and said, "I've got some things to do for a little while. Plus, it may be better said in private." He looked down at her and cracked a small smile. He was easily a half a foot taller than her and she looked up, met his eyes and smiled herself. He removed her hand from his arm, walked out into the hall and down to his office and closed the door behind him. He pulled out his cell phone and dialed a number.

“Kohler,” Jon started, “What’s going on?

There was a pause on the other end of the line before Kohler answered. “Ah, we lost them for now.”

“What the hell do you mean, you lost them?”

“Just that, sorry. We need two vehicles sir. The girl left this morning by herself so we stayed with Layton’s car. The kid and the old man slept there all night so we figured they were still in the house.”

“Where’d they go?”

“That’s the thing, we don’t know. After an hour of waiting, Pierce busted in and they were gone. Must’ve slipped out the back.”

“Why didn’t one of you cover it?”

“It was broad daylight sir; we couldn’t just snoop around people’s backyards.”

“Dammit!”

“Sir, they’ll be back. The kid’s car is still here and plus, we’re meeting him tonight at his house where he has to hand it over. Speaking of which, what is it that you want so bad? It’s a book right?”

Castle debated for a few moments. At first he didn’t want to tell them. The less people that knew about what he was up to the better. But now, with more people coming into the mix, he wanted that book first. “Yes, it’s a book,” Castle said.

“What kind of book?” Kohler asked.

“Just an old book, that’s all.”

“You’re sure going to a lot of trouble for a book,” Kohler said.

“It’s not just any book, Kohler,” Castle angrily said. “It’s a book that could lead to…to, something.”

"What kind of something?" Kohler asked insistently.

"Don't worry about it for now. You'll be handsomely compensated when you find it."

"Fine. We're still parked outside the girl's house. If they don't come back here in the next few hours we're going to head over to the kid's house. You sure you don't wanna bring more people in on this, cover both houses?"

"No, two is enough. If you can't get the job done, I will find replacements."

"Okay, okay. We'll keep you posted."

"Wait," Castle said into the phone. He stood up from his chair and looked out the window overlooking Massachusetts Avenue. "We have some guests coming…uninvited guests."

"Huh, what do you mean guests?"

"Let's just say there is someone else interested in this book and they will also do anything to get their hands on it."

"Who is it?" Kohler asked.

"That doesn't matter for now. Just be on the lookout. They know the kid may have found it and they are coming in sometime. They may already be there."

"Coming in, from where?" Kohler said.

So many questions. "From the UK, alright? From the goddamned UK!"

"Jeez, okay sir, we'll do our best."

"I don't want any trouble okay? Whoever finds it, great. But in all honesty, I want first dibs on that book. Get back to work."

Castle closed the phone and placed it on his desk.

He took off his sport coat and tossed it on the maroon leather couch. Hands on his hips, he paced behind his desk staring out the window. He checked his watch and it was after noon. "Eh, what the hell" he said softly. He sat down, opened his bottom drawer and pulled out his work stash, another bottle of Jim Beam. He brought his white coffee cup down below his desk and poured just a little. It was finished quickly and the bottle was put away back in the drawer.

CHAPTER 11

The Atwater Kent Museum was dedicated in 1941 after three years of construction. The mayor of Philadelphia at the time, S. Davis Wilson, brought the idea to Kent along with Francis Wistar, president of the Philadelphia Society for the Preservation of Landmarks. Today, the museum was home to over 80,000 objects related to Philadelphia and the surrounding area. These consisted of everything from the Quakers of the 17th Century, to 18th Century art, to Philadelphia manufacturing of the 19th and 20th Century.

Seth and Madison were glad to walk off the heavy lunch they had, but all Arthur wanted to do was take a nap. The beer and the burger put him into a nutritional coma and he trailed behind as they approached the museum. The first brochure that was handed to them outside the door revealed that the museum had been closed for the past eighteen months and just reopened a few weeks ago. It was renamed The Philadelphia

History Museum at The Atwater Kent.

"You want us to drive you home, Granddad?" Seth asked, watching Arthur slowly pull up the rear.

Arthur waved his hand at him in disgust. "Drive? Son, before your day, all we did was walk. Miles and miles every day. I'm fine."

There was no ornate landscaping or large grass field leading up to the museum; in fact it looked like a huge church. The building was a large, drab, concrete monstrosity. Light posts stood atop small stone pillars that guarded the entrance to large double doors made of dark maple. Seth opened the door on his right and held it for Madison and Arthur to walk through.

They paid their admission fee and followed the masses to the inside of the building and took in the sights. Pictures and plaques adorned every wall. Glass cases housed hundreds of years of Philadelphia history. They were on a mission to find the Betsy Ross House renovation so they didn't take much time to stop and stare at the interesting pieces of art. Seth did stop at the Philadelphia Sports' Fan exhibit. Pictures of fans celebrating victories were displayed in a huge collage. Stadiums, the new, like Citizens Bank Park, and old, like Connie Mack Stadium were shown throughout a timeline going back one hundred years.

"Pretty cool, eh Granddad?" Seth said.

Arthur came up behind and they just scanned the photos for a few brief moments until Madison grabbed them by their shirts and pulled them along. Fifteen minutes later, they completed their tour of the museum without finding anything of significance.

"Now what? Another dead end?" Seth asked.

"Wait here," Madison said. She walked over to a small portly man standing guard at the entrance. Although he wore a blue shirt and black pants, he had no gun, no handcuffs and no nightstick, just a small radio and a can of pepper spray attached to his belt. He did not see much excitement in his ten to five job, but, he noticed Madison right away as she walked toward him, taking the clip out of her blonde hair and letting it fall to her shoulders. She also took off her jean jacket and folded it under her arm. Now, the guard couldn't help himself from glancing down at her chest as she got close.

"Hey there, Mitch," she said, reading the name on his nameplate. He had an oversized blue baseball cap on that covered what Madison thought was a comb over of his black hair.

"Yes?" the man stammered.

"Is this everything you have?" she asked, waving her arm around the large atrium.

"Um, yes ma'am," he replied.

"I mean everything?" she said softly. "What about items Mr. Kent had that didn't make it into the museum? There's nothing in some warehouse?"

"Well, there are some," he said, looking around nervously. "One time, I found an old comic book collection, over twenty of them." Mitch was excited now and his sentences ran together. "They were in great condition too. Mr. Parcels wouldn't let me have them, though. He said they belonged to the museum. I said, 'what good are they sitting down here in the basement'. Can't stand that guy." He looked around again, hoping no one heard him.

"Basement? There's a basement here?" Madison asked.

"Sure."

"Can I see it?" Madison asked.

"Oh no, no, no. Mr. Parcels wouldn't like that. He wouldn't like that one bit. He wouldn't." Mitch looked around again. "I've been down there though. Couple of times, I have. Why do you want to go down there anyway? You shouldn't go down there."

Madison leaned in close so that her breasts were inches from Mitch's right arm. "Mr. Parcels sounds like a jerk, Mitch," she said.

Mitch froze.

"He is a jerk, isn't he Mitch?" Madison said.

Mitch nodded his head up and down rather quickly.

"How about you break the rules a little bit today? I'd love for you to show me the basement, Mitch." This time her right breast pressed into his arm ever so slightly.

Mitch reached into his pants pocket and brought out a large set of keys. "Follow me," he said.

Madison looked over at Arthur and Seth, snapped her fingers and tilted her head in her direction. Mitch led her down a small hallway that had a sign that read, "Employees Only". He stopped at the third door on the right and looked both ways before unlocking the door and escorting Madison inside. Mitch flipped on a light switch and the small enclosure was illuminated. The only thing that could be seen was stairs leading down. Before he closed the door behind them, Seth and Arthur walked in.

"Hey, you can't come in here!" Mitch exclaimed.

"It's okay," Madison said, "they're with me."

"What's going on here?" Mitch inquired, his right hand on a can of pepper spray.

"It's nothing. Bill here is my brother," Madison lied, "and this is my grandfather, Earl. My grandfather's father told him that he etched his name somewhere on Betsy Ross' house almost a hundred years ago and we wanna see if he's telling the truth. We already checked the house and we were told that some of the original framework was here."

Mitch looked at each of their eyes, looking for doubt but could not find any. He led them down the stairs. It was narrow and the stairs turned on a right angle every seven or eight steps.

"How do you get the stuff up here being that the stairs are so narrow?" Madison asked.

"There's a gigantic trap door over the third wing. We have a forklift down here that will just lift the new display up."

They reached the bottom of the staircase and Mitch once again flicked a light switch. In front of them was a long narrow path with chain-linked cages on each side. Each cage was connected to one another and had a six foot door of identical fence. Both were padlocked. Inside the first cage were various paintings of different sizes leaning against the back wall. On the door to the cage was a small brown envelope attached by a thin rope.

"Thomas Eakins," Mitch said. They slowed their pace and looked in the cage as they continued walking. "So, you're looking for the Betsy Ross renovation, eh? Not sure what you're looking for is down here, but I remember seeing it when I was given a tour of the place on my first day."

The four of them continued walking down the center of the walkway, occasionally slowing as they approached some sort of famous Philadelphia history and listening to Mitch explain the artifacts inside the cage. About halfway through, Mitch stopped outside of a cage and brought out his janitor-sized key chain.

"Here ya go…the Betsy Ross renovation."

Madison grabbed his arm after he unlocked the door and said, "Mitch, let's see what else is down here."

He looked at Seth and Arthur, then back at her and couldn't resist her smile. "Don't touch anything until I get back," he said. Madison continued walking and Mitch caught up to her and escorted her, continuing down the walkway.

Seth and Arthur walked into the small cage. It was deeper than it appeared. At ten feet in width, the cage stretched almost twenty feet to the back wall. There were some pictures on the floor, a dresser, a bed frame and two rocking chairs on either side of the cage. Against the back wall they finally found it, the staircase. It was separated into three sections, each consisting of about five steps. The wood was dark and grainy but in relatively good shape for being over two-hundred years old.

"According to the drawing, we need to find the sixth step," Seth said. He lifted the second set of steps, careful not to make a lot of noise, and turned the fragile wood over. The back of each step had another piece of wood nailed in placed to form a type of box. Seth found the sixth step and this one looked the same as the others, except for a small hinge on either side and a rusty clasp at the top.

"This is it," Arthur said. His eyes grew in excitement. "Go ahead, son."

Seth reached up and unhooked the clasp. Nothing happened. After many years the wood had settled and it was snug on either side. Seth couldn't get a good grip to pull open the box. Arthur reached into his pocket and pulled out a small Swiss Army knife. "Always comes in handy," he said, handing Seth the knife.

He flicked it open and inserted the knife in the top and started to wedge the top down and open.

"Wow, that's great." Madison's voice echoed though the hallway.

"They're coming back! Hurry," Arthur said.

Seth pulled open the back of the step and saw a small dark blanket stuffed inside. He tugged on the cloth, pulling it from its hiding spot and tearing a few strands of thread on the wood. The voices were closer now. He didn't want the security guy to see he had taken something so with no other choice; he lifted up his shirt and stuffed the blanket inside. They both hurried out of the small cage and shut the door behind them as Madison and Mitch came toward them.

"Find anything?" Mitch asked.

"Nah, must've been an old wives' tale," Seth said, nodding his head toward the exit at Madison. His hands were folded across his stomach, partially hiding the bulge in his shirt.

"You didn't touch anything did ya?" Mitch asked, peering inside the gate as he relocked it.

Madison grabbed Mitch's arm and led him towards

the steps. "Thanks Mitch, I really appreciate you letting us come down here."

"Sure, I mean, sure, anytime. Hey do you want to get a cup of coffee?" Mitch asked Madison.

They walked up the stairs as Madison responded, "Um, I think grandfather is feeling a little tired."

"I feel fine," Arthur said as they reached the top of the stairs.

Seth gave him a polite tap in the ribs and Arthur quickly changed his mind. "Actually I could probably use a little nap."

Disappointed, Mitch escorted them out the door and the three of them hurried down the steps and found Madison's car in the nearby parking garage. Seth let Arthur take the front seat while he sat in the back and they caught their breath for a few moments.

"Well," Madison asked, "did you find anything?"

Seth pulled up his shirt and the navy blanket fell to his lap. It was definitely old and musty and smelled like it. The blanket was rolled up tight. He unwrapped the blanket, rolling it down his legs to the floor.

There it was. A small pouch similar to Washington's journal rested at the bottom of the blanket. This pouch was longer and flatter and it was folded in half. Seth looked out the car windows to see if anyone was watching.

"Hurry up already!" Arthur said, turning in his seat to watch him.

Seth unfolded the brown leather satchel and untied the small knot in the front. He peered inside and reached his hand in. He pulled out a rolled up piece of leather, again tied with small knot of twine. Untying that he finally found a piece of yellow-stained paper that was also rolled long ways. It was brittle and he was afraid it would disintegrate in his hands.

"Just be careful," Madison said.

He didn't respond, but gave her a look that indicated he knew to be careful. He started unraveling the paper and found words neatly written in black ink.

"Read it!" Arthur said.

March 14th, 1800

The day started out slightly chilly, but it was time to set off. Bushrod had waited for the winter to pass before he made the long trek to Philadelphia. He did not want to be caught in a Nor'easter with nothing but him and his horse to keep him warm. His horse, Willow, would only be able to go about fifty miles a day, so it took Bushrod and Willow three days to reach his destination.

Soon after the burial of his uncle George, he spent many days talking to his aunt Martha about what his uncle had hidden in Philadelphia. After scouring through his journal, Bushrod figured out the location, but Martha would not tell him about the hidden contents. For months he wondered what must be hidden in the document and here he was standing on the front porch of Miss Betsy Ross's house.

He knocked twice and waited patiently for the woman to open to the door.

"Yes," a woman said while opening the door. For someone in their late forties, Miss Ross looked exceptionally well. Touches of gray and black hair peeked out from her bonnet. She was certainly full-figured which Bushrod didn't mind. Bushrod himself was thirty-eight at the time and he had planned to use his trim build and good looks to charm the woman.

"Miss Ross? Hello, I've traveled quite far to meet with you. Do you have a moment?"

"Um, yes, come in." She pushed open the door and Bushrod followed her in. "Who are you?"

"This is quite a nice place you have," Bushrod said.

"Thank you," she replied.

He took her arms in his hands. "I am George Washington's nephew."

She removed her left hand to cover her mouth. "Oh, I'm so sorry for your loss. Mr. Washington was the bravest of all souls. You know, George and I used to attend church services together. He and I had a special relationship. He will be terribly missed."

"It's okay, thank you. He lived a great life and left us a country that will last for ages."

"So, what brings you here? Oh I know!" she said.

"Yes," Bushrod agreed.

"I don't know where it is, actually. He told me to leave the house and said that he was hiding something very important and that if anyone came to get it outside his family, I was to tell them it was a lie."

Bushrod held up Washington's journal. "I think I know where it is."

They both found the sixth step rather quickly and Bushrod unraveled the blanket and pulled out a large scroll of paper filled with words from top to bottom. After reading it, he rolled it back up and stuck it in his own satchel. He was shocked to say the least but he did not let Betsy Ross read the document.

"What are you doing?" Ross asked.

"I'm taking it," he responded. "It's too valuable to sit in this house which could burn down one day or be ransacked and looted. I will take this to a more secure place. Do you have paper and a quill?"

She did and Bushrod composed his own note:

To those seeking what's hidden in this house, I have moved it to a more secure location not far from here. If you are worthy, you will know that place is where my Uncle left a legacy during an important winter that changed the course of this great country.

Bushrod Washington

CHAPTER 12

"That's it?" Arthur asked. "That's all it says?"

Seth paused and re-read the brief note, confirming that was all it said. He turned the brittle parchment paper over and looked for any other words of significance. There was nothing written on the other side. He went through the satchel, searching each and every pocket, looking for something else, anything that could help them. It was empty. Frustrated, he tossed the bag to his granddad and said, "That's it."

"Twenty-five years and to think we finally solved the puzzle," Arthur said, frustrated.

Madison started the car and pulled out of the garage. After she paid the parking attendant with a credit card, she pulled onto 5th Street and headed out of the city, via route 676. The traffic was building as it was nearing rush hour.

"Well?" Seth asked, looking at Madison in the rear-view mirror.

She looked back and replied, "Well, what?"

"Aren't you going to say something?"

A small smile formed on her lips. "I'm waiting for you to figure it out."

"Figure what out?" Arthur asked.

"You guys are so pissed off that we didn't find whatever it is we're looking for, you failed to solve the next clue."

A black sports car passed them on the left going at least eighty miles per hour.

Arthur turned in his seat and said, "Read it again, son."

Seth unraveled the scroll and read aloud, "To those seeking what's hidden in this house, I have moved it to a more secure location not far from here. If you are worthy, you will know that place is where my Uncle left a legacy through an important winter that changed the course of this great country."

Arthur smiled and turned to Madison, "Good work, my dear."

"Shit, Valley Forge," Seth said from the back. "That's only twenty minutes from here. I did a research paper on Valley Forge in college for a history class."

"Good," Madison replied, "We're going there first thing in the morning."

Madison dropped Arthur off at Harper's Grove. They were going to keep him for the night, but he was already snoring in his seat and he needed the rest. Seth didn't even want him coming tomorrow, but there was no way to keep Arthur away from the chase they were on. Fifteen minutes later they pulled into Seth's condominium complex and Seth and Madison got out of the car. They'd decided to stay at Seth's because they knew Madison's was probably still being watched. Seth also had the deadline to worry about. He was supposed to produce the book to whoever those men were by 8 pm.

Seth pulled out his key and was about to stick it in the door, but the door was ajar. He pulled Madison behind him and opened the door. Immediately, he saw that his place was trashed. Seth pushed the door all the way open and stepped inside. It was eerily quiet for all of the destruction in the house. In the kitchen to the right everything had been dumped out of his cabinets and drawers. Cereal boxes, pasta and pretzels lay on the floor as the cabinets were completely cleaned out.

"Holy crap," Madison said. "I knew you weren't that tidy, Seth, but I didn't know you were a slob," she said, trying to make light of the situation.

Seth turned his head and gave her a "not now" look.

"Sorry."

"I think we know who did this," Seth said, closing the door behind him and now stepping into the living room. The cushions on the couch were overturned, the CD's and DVD's strewn about the floor. They continued into the bedroom and found the same mess. All of his clothes were out of the drawers and off the hangers in the closet. The mattress was stripped and overturned, laying half on the bed and half on the floor.

"Jeez, Seth, what is so important about this book?"

"I have no idea," he replied. A thought came to him. "Maybe we should just give it to them."

"What?"

"Even if they figure out the clues, they won't find anything. You think they're smart enough to go to the Betsy Ross house? And if they do, there's nothing there. They won't determine the renovation remains are in the Atwater Kent Museum. If they miraculously figure that out, there's nothing there either. We took the satchel."

"Seth, based on the threat from last night, these guys are either cops, or worse, the feds."

"You think?"

"I don't know, but they sure appear to be. If they were gangsters, we'd be dead or in the hospital by now. If we followed the trail, they certainly can. It will still lead back to us. They'll know we found something and they'll never leave us alone."

"True," Seth thought. "But that will take time and it'll give us a head start to Valley Forge."

Madison looked around the trashed bedroom. "Hope they didn't do this to my place. Let's go."

<><><><><>

"Alright, here's the plan," Max began. "Evan, I'm going to drop you off around the back in case they try and run for it. Chloe and I will confront them as they get out of the car."

"Why do I have to be the one in the back? Because she's a woman, she can't do it alone?"

"Screw you, Evan," Chloe replied. "It's because you'll fuck it up is why."

"Shut it you two," Max interjected. "This is the plan. And besides," he said with a smile at Chloe, "you probably would screw it up Evan."

"Go to bloody hell, the both of you," Evan said from the backseat.

"Now, Chloe and I will approach them and ask for the book. If they give us any trouble, we'll handle it."

"What about the local boys staking out the house?" Chloe asked.

"I'll deal with them," Max responded.

They continued driving until they were in Madison's neighborhood. Max turned the Pathfinder onto the street behind Madison's house and dropped Evan off. They made their way around the block and pulled up in front of the house as Seth and Madison exited the car. Max and Chloe got out of the car and walked across the front lawn.

"Excuse me," Max said, rather loudly.

Seth turned to the man and woman coming across the grass and grabbed Madison's hand. He had no idea who they were, but with all that had happened in the past forty-eight hours, he wasn't taking any chances. He picked up his pace and tried to make it to the front door before they could reach them. Madison fumbled with her keys and turned to see the couple just ten feet away. They were not going to make it.

"I got her," Chloe whispered. As soon as the woman was near enough, Madison swung her purse high at the woman's head. She was too slow. The other woman ducked and grabbed it when it descended, pulling hard and sending Madison to the ground. Seth caught this out of the corner of his eye as he stood his ground, waiting for his attacker to strike.

"Don't be stupid, Seth," Max said, opening his

sport coat ever so slightly and revealing the Glock he had in his waistband.

A puzzling look came across Seth's brow. *A gun? How did he know my name?*

"Don't hurt her," Seth said.

"We're not going to hurt anyone as long as we get what we want," Max said.

Madison got up off the ground and was handed the purse from the red-haired woman. She took it and stood next to Seth. "Who are you?" she asked.

Before Max had a chance to answer, two car doors closed from across the street. They all turned and saw two men exit the SUV and approach Madison's house.

"Here come the Yanks," Max said to Chloe.

The two men walked up the driveway and stopped about fifteen feet away from them. The bald one smiled, elbowed his partner and spoke first, "Ah, our friends from across the pond. Guess we're gonna take it from here, mates."

Max chuckled. "You got it wrong, *mate*. You couldn't handle this bloody mess so we gotta clean it up. Move along, we got it."

Pierce stepped forward a few feet, twisting a toothpick that hung from his mouth. "What, you and your little girlfriend there gonna handle me and my partner?"

"We won't just handle you," Chloe said, "We'll beat ya to a bloody pulp."

Pierce made a move forward, but he was stopped by his partner's outstretched arm. "Let's be civil about this and get what we want, the book."

Max disagreed, "That book is leaving with us." He

looked at Seth and said, "Hand it over."

"You're not taking it anywhere," Kohler said. "It stays with us."

Seth looked over at Madison while the four of them argued. If they ever had a chance, now was it. He moved his eyes over to her car then down to the keys still in her right hand, not saying anything. Reaching into his backpack, he removed a small box. Seth then flashed five fingers on his hand and waited until she looked down and saw them. He slowly peeled a finger down, showing four, then three, then two…

"You want the book?" Seth shouted. "Here it is!" He took the small box, which now contained the journal, and side-armed it across the lawn away from the driveway. The moment the words came out of his mouth, Madison ran to the car. Seth followed.

The three men and one woman scrambled to the box lying thirty feet away. Halfway there, Chloe stopped and turned to see Madison in the front seat of the car and Seth opening the door. She drew her weapon. "Freeze!"

The threat fell on deaf ears. Madison started the car and Seth closed the passenger door. Chloe didn't want to fire, not in a suburban neighborhood. Plus, if the book was actually in the box, they were no longer needed. She turned. Her partner had grabbed the overweight guy in the suit and flung him backward. Kohler and Max jumped on the box. She turned back and saw the car backing out of the driveway. Just then, her other partner Evan came running down the driveway from the back of the house. As the car reached the street and Madison shifted into drive, Evan dove on top of the car, grasping at the car where the hood met the windshield.

Madison screamed and stepped on the gas.

After fifty feet, the man was still holding onto the car.

"Brake!" Seth yelled.

She did and the man tumbled from the roof onto the street, rolling side over side toward the curb. She quickly hit the gas again and the car peeled out of sight.

Chloe ran to the street still clutching her gun with both hands. A neighbor from across the street turned on a light and stepped out onto his front porch. Chloe holstered the weapon and trotted over to where Evan lay writhing in pain.

"You okay?" she asked.

"You shoulda shot the bastards," he said through clenched teeth.

She helped him up and they walked back to the house. Kohler ended up with the book and Pierce was pointing his gun at Max, who still lay on the ground.

"Put it away dipshit," Max said. "You wanna get us all pinched?" Chloe approached and reached for her own weapon. "Don't," he said. He got to his feet and straightened his jacket. Kohler peeled off the rubber bands and opened the box. He reached inside and pulled out the journal.

"Okay, you won this one," Max said to the man holding the box while rising to his feet. "Now, do you wanna be smart with this or just go run back to Castle and tell him you found it?"

Kohler looked at him. "Our job was to find this book, that's it. We're done here."

"Think about it," Max said, brushing his shirt to remove the blades of grass. "Why would they give you the book? There's either nothing in it, or they found what's in it and have it in their possession. Gentlemen," he said quietly, "the book is only step one. We need to find what the book tells us to find."

Kohler and Pierce exchanged puzzled looks. "What do you mean?"

"I mean, that book is only the first clue in finding out the real prize your boss is searching for. Frankly, it's what my boss was searching for too."

"What do you suggest?" Kohler asked.

"We work together," Max said.

"Ahh, now we gotta work with these incompetent Yanks?" Evan said.

"Quiet," Max said. He pointed at the book. "If you take that book back to Castle and there's nothing there, he's gonna keep sending you on a wild goose chase."

Kohler stretched his neck from side to side before responding. "So now what?"

"We'll split up. You guys take off and we'll watch both places, here and the kid's place. They gotta stay somewhere for the night, although I doubt it's either one of these places. So, use your connections and get a tail on all credit card purchases in the next twenty four hours. I bet they find a hotel and shack up there for the night. If you find out which one, we got 'em."

"I'm keeping the book though," Kohler said.

"Deal." Max reached forward and shook the reluctant hand of the man with the book.

CHAPTER 13

The sun had disappeared from the horizon, but the last quarter of the sky had a pinkish hue that mesmerized those looking west. Contrails of exhaust from jetliners crisscrossed each other like they were playing a game of tag, their plumes expanding as they went further toward their destinations. Seth looked up at them through the front windshield of Madison's car and wished he was on one of those planes right now. He'd scoop up his granddad and take him with him, Madison too, he hoped. Where to go? Endless possibilities. Couldn't go to Florida to see his father, they'd track him there. Tahiti?

"Where to?" Madison asked. She breezed through stop signs and anticipated green lights as she made her way onto Interstate 476, going north toward Valley Forge. They couldn't go there now; any attractions in the park would be closed. "Seth!"

"Oh, sorry," Seth said, crashing back to reality after

his brief Tahitian excursion. "I still can't figure out who those other people were."

"They had British accents too. And that man who jumped on my car! Geez. What the hell do they want?"

"Beats me, but we gotta find out." For the first few minutes after their escape, they summarized the events and knew that the knowledge they had was valuable.

"Where are we going?" she asked.

"Well, we can't go to your place or my place. I was thinking my granddad's abandoned house but they found me there before so that's out. We could stay at a friend's place," he said it almost as a question.

She thought for a moment before saying, "I don't want to get anyone else involved in this, let alone get hurt."

"Then it's a hotel."

"Okay," she said, "which one?"

"I want to be there as soon as Valley Forge Park opens tomorrow morning so let's stay somewhere close. Go to the Radisson, it's right near the park. Take I-76 all the way to King of Prussia and it's right off Route 23."

The journey to the Radisson in rush hour traffic took about thirty minutes. Seth relayed his thoughts about his research paper on Valley Forge to Madison. Washington had chosen Valley Forge as an interim position for the winter of 1777. It was perched high on a hill and the Schuylkill River was nearby, both helping their defense. He led 12,000 men into the area and they built over one thousand log cabins to help them stave off winter's fury. Still, almost 2000 men died of typhoid, jaundice, pneumonia and dysentery.

"Were there any women in the camp?" Madison asked.

"Sure, wives, children, mothers and sisters were there. Only a couple hundred of them, but they provided laundry, cooking and even nursing services. They were even scavengers of some sort. After a minor battle, they would run out to the battlefield and try to take whatever was on the dead soldiers' body and bring it back to the camp. Some even got killed doing it."

"How long were the soldiers there?"

"They left when summer arrived, sometime in June. But to this day, it is considered a monumental victory of morale in the war. They suffered through a very harsh winter and Washington instilled in his men that if they could survive that, they could survive anything."

"So where are we going to find whatever it is that's hidden?"

"I have some ideas, but the park is huge. It's over three thousand acres."

"We'll never find it," Madison said.

"Well, most of it is just grass and trees, walking and biking paths too. You're right, if it's buried in the ground, it will be almost impossible to find. We need to look for something that has endured the test of time."

Madison pulled into the parking lot of the Radisson and they got out and walked to the front desk. A tall skinny man with a light gray suit stood standing behind the chest-high counter. His gold nameplate said his name was William.

"Hello and welcome to the Radisson," the man said. "How can I help you?"

Seth spoke first, "Yes we need a room for," he

caught himself and said, “ah, two rooms.”

Madison grabbed his hand and said to William, “One room is fine.”

William smiled before typing on the computer on the desk. “We have a room available with one king-sized bed. Will that be okay?”

“Yes,” Madison said, “that will be fine.”

Seth smiled and pulled out his credit card. They got the room key from William and walked toward the elevators and room 416.

“We need to eat something,” Seth said. “Where should we go?”

Madison locked arms with him and smiled. Room service.”

Jonathon Castle’s cell phone rang in his office. He was sitting at his desk and his assistant, Kim, sat across from him taking notes, her glasses creeping down her nose. Castle looked at the caller ID and got up from his chair.

“Excuse me,” he said. He walked around his desk to the far corner and said, “Yes?”

“We ran into the people from the UK,” the man on the other end said. It was Kohler.

“And?” Castle asked, trying not to give too much away to his assistant.

“We got the book.”

“Excellent! What about the two who had it?”

“That’s the thing. The guy sorta gave it to us.”

“What? You didn’t have to…” Castle searched for the words, “take it?”

"No," Kohler stated. "We went through the book and there's not much here. Couple of drawings but I couldn't make anything out of it."

"I see," Castle said.

"We think the kid knows something or else he wouldn't have handed it over so easy."

"Where are they?"

"We just got a hit. We put a trail on their credit card and they checked into the Radisson near King of Prussia. We got them under surveillance."

"Great," Castle said. "Keep me posted. I'll call you later." He ended the call and smiled. He had the book. Better yet, maybe the kid found what he was looking for after all and that would soon be his as well. Things were looking up.

It was getting late and he figured they were the last two people on this floor. He put the phone in his pocket and walked behind Kim, still sitting in front of his desk. He put his hands on her shoulders and started gently massaging.

Kim was not taken off guard. She eased into the massage, gently rolling her neck in small circles. No words were spoken and soon Kim got up from her chair, locked his office door and moved over to the leather sofa against the wall, grabbing his hand as she walked. Castle unbuttoned his shirt with his left hand and she unbuttoned her white blouse with her right hand. She turned to face him, looking up in his eyes. Then she undid his pants as he undid her skirt, both falling to the floor. In no time they were fully undressed and he was on top of her, crashing onto the couch.

"Oh Kim," Castle said, whispering into her ear.

Kim whispered right back, “Oh Mr. Vice-President.”

CHAPTER 14

Morning came quickly for Seth and Madison. Both were exhausted from the previous day's activities. Coffee was brought to their room at eight o'clock along with two bagels and cream cheese. They made two quick phone calls. Seth called his granddad to let him know they'd be by later, and Madison called work to say she wouldn't be in again. They showered, redressed in the same clothes and headed out the door, breakfast in hand.

It was a bright, crisp spring morning and the cool breeze was refreshing. Madison drove the short distance to the entrance of Valley Forge Park and parked the car in the lot near the Visitor's Center. It opened at nine and they wanted to be the first customers through the doors.

They walked up a concrete path toward the glass building that seemed to be sitting inside the side of a hill. Joggers and bikers breezed by them on the wide trail that encircled the park.

"Hi folks," a small elderly man said standing behind the counter.

Seth grabbed a map from the counter stand and asked the man, "Hi. We're curious to know what exists here in the park that existed back in Washington's day?"

"What do you mean son?"

Seth cleared his throat and clarified. "I'm wondering what buildings or structures are still standing and unchanged after two hundred and some odd years."

"Oh," the man said as he grabbed the map from Seth's hands and opened it. "Here we are," he pointed at the map, "The oldest buildings are The Stevens House right here and Varnum's Quarter's over here. Down here you got Knox's Quarters, and then up here you have Washington's Quarters. Plus a few huts still remain and they are scattered around the whole park."

Seth and Madison looked at each other. They knew where to look first. Seth folded the map back, thanked the man, grabbed Madison's hand and exited the Center.

"Washington's Quarters," he said.

"Got to be," she replied.

They walked back to Madison's car and noticed another car sitting on the other side of the parking lot. Seth could tell the car was idling because there was gray smoke coming from the exhaust pipe on the back of the car.

"They followed us," he said, looking away, searching for a plan. "We can't walk there, too easy to follow us. We have to lose them. Get in."

They climbed in the car and Madison pulled out

and found Route 23. She accelerated and turned onto the outer drive. She drove the opposite way of Washington's Quarters, hoping to lead them astray. Madison glanced in the rearview mirror; the car turned out and wasn't far behind.

"Shit, they're behind us. How'd they find us?"

Seth peered in his mirror and confirmed it. "Get on route 252, then take 202 South. We can loop around and try to lose them."

Madison did as Seth suggested, and after four miles, she didn't see the car behind them anymore. What she also didn't see was the red flashing light that was mounted under her car that was tracking her every turn.

Vice-President Jonathon Castle was cruising toward the mid-way point of his third year of his first term in office. He'd lost the Republican Primary to the current President, Richard Bowe, but it was so close, they both agreed they would win the election in a landslide if they were running mates. This was not all that common but the voters swarmed to the polls and pulled the lever for Bowe/Castle.

Although he welcomed the idea of being VP, Castle was still upset that he didn't sleep in the White House. Instead, he sat a few miles away in his home office in the U.S. Naval Observatory. After carousing with his assistant Kim the night before, he retired to the third floor, took a shower, and then crawled into bed with his wife, who barely noticed him. He figured she probably knew something was going on, but he didn't give a damn. She was not going to ruin his political career. Doing so, she would say goodbye to all of the fancy corporate dinners at the White House, the private jets all over the world and the endless campaign money that flooded in.

That morning he was preparing for a meeting in his office when his private cell phone rang and he saw that it was Kohler. Another update.

Castle spoke first, "What've you got?"

"They spent the night in the hotel then made their way to Valley Forge Park first thing."

"Valley Forge?" Castle asked inquisitively.

"Yeah, they stopped at the Visitor's Center then I think they made us. They drove around for fifteen minutes trying to lose us."

"Dammit Kohler!" Castle snapped.

"Don't worry sir," Kohler said calmly. "We put a bug on their car in the parking lot of the hotel last night. They're not going anywhere without us knowing it."

"Where's the other three jerk-offs from the UK?"

"They are stationed at the two houses."

"Good," Castle said. "Keep them guessing. I will handle Bannister. Keep your distance from Layton and the girl too. I don't want him to make you again and not pursue what I want."

"Okay," Kohler responded.

"Where are they now?"

"They drove around in circles for a little bit and we let them go. We got the laptop up right now and they're close to the park again. Looks like they're headed toward a building. Zoom in right there," Kohler said to his partner who was holding the laptop. "Yep, looks like they just parked near a building called Washington's Quarters. What is that?"

"That, Agent Kohler, means they're close. Keep me posted." Castle ended the call and looked out the window of his office with a smile on his face. *They're close*, he thought.

CHAPTER 15

General George Washington, although living with his thousands of men, did not sleep in a tent or a wooden hut at Valley Forge. He had a traditional brick house that he shared at the time with his wife Martha. It was originally built for Isaac Potts, operator of the family grist mill in the mid to late 1700's. It wasn't until 1972 that it was declared a National Landmark. Seth finished reading the pamphlet and stared at the house in front of them

It looked to be a typical farmhouse, even to this day. It was a two-story building with three windows on the top and two on the bottom, along with a door positioned awkwardly on the left side. Around that corner of the house and sitting back was an additional one-story building that to Seth looked like a small barn or workshop. The overhang between the two structures connected them so one would not get rained or snowed upon while walking between the two buildings.

Seth looked in every direction and didn't see the car that had followed them. There were only a few other people here at this hour, but he could see a school bus pulling into the lot.

"Let's go," he said to Madison. "This place will be crawling with little kids in a few minutes."

"Not a bad distraction," Madison said softly.

They walked up to the main door and were greeted by an elderly woman with long hair, a tattered but flowing gown and glasses perched on the end of her nose. She looked like the character they saw yesterday impersonating Betsy Ross.

"Greetings, please, please, come in. I am Martha Washington and welcome to my humble abode." She raised her arm out to the side and let them walk in.

Seth and Madison walked through the doorway, Seth almost bumping his head. Everything seemed very small and cramped. They were ushered to their right and followed another older couple on a tour of the house. They saw the kitchen, Washington's study, and various bedrooms. Interestingly, to make the home seem more real, there were the General's uniforms, boots, socks, and other clothes strewn about over chairs in the bedroom. It was almost like Washington had just come back from battle.

"Excuse me," Seth asked. "Did any of Washington's relatives ever come to his house here at Valley Forge?"

"Well not during the war. No, it was too dangerous." Martha replied.

"What about after the war?"

"I couldn't say for sure, but there would be no

record of anyone visiting. There'd be no reason to and the place was given to another family. Why do you ask?"

"Just curious is all."

March 14th, 1800

Bushrod was tired from his long journey to Philadelphia. He hadn't bothered to stay the night, as he wanted to get the document hidden safely away in his uncle's house at Valley Forge. It was nearing dark and he was lost. His horse, Willow, stopped to take a drink from the rainwater that started to accumulate in small puddles on the trail.

They were both cold as the rain started to come down harder. He heard movement to his right through the thicket of trees. Riding horseback in the dark was dangerous enough. He didn't need wild animals or something worse to keep him from his mission. Bushrod pulled on the reigns to get Willow to start moving again. Reluctantly, the horse did as commanded and they trotted through the woods.

Bushrod heard the noise again to his right. It sounded like someone or something was following them. It was more than one animal or one person. There were at least two of them. Bushrod kicked his heels at Willow and they picked up their pace. Just then, two men came running out of the woods toward Bushrod. One held a slingshot and the other a handful of large stones. The man pulled back on the slingshot and released a large stone at the head of Bushrod. He saw it in the nick of time and ducked, and the stone grazed the back of his head.

He raced through the trees and heard the men laughing behind him as he pulled away. Willow went full stride for another fifteen minutes before Bushrod willed him to a stop. He recognized where he was, near the banks of the Delaware River. They were in the complete opposite direction of Valley Forge. He thought about it and decided to forgo the trip to his uncle's quarters, promising to leave the document there on his next visit to Philadelphia. So instead, he made the long journey back home. The document was still in his possession.

Once again they were cut off from exploring anything deeper due to the staff inside the house. Ropes lined the doors and other tourists roamed about which made a thorough search impossible. Seth was frustrated and held his head in his hands as they exited the building.

"Cripes, now what?" Seth asked.

Madison yawned and stretched her arms over her head before responding. "We find out where the hell this Bushrod lived, died or whatever. He took something from the Ross house and hid it. Supposedly here. Where? I have no idea. Maybe he moved it again. We need to find out everything we can about

Bushrod Washington."

"For what?" Seth asked quickly.

Madison looked over at him as they made their way toward the car. He didn't return her gaze but kept staring ahead. "Are you done?" she asked.

He shrugged and put his hands in his jacket pockets. "I mean, what's the point?"

"I'm not gonna argue with you anymore, Seth. We had this same conversation yesterday and you said you were in. I'll drop you off at the hotel or your place or wherever you wanna go."

Seth gazed in every direction as they neared the car and saw no sign of the vehicle that followed them earlier that day. "What are you going to do?"

"I don't know yet," she responded. "Maybe see where Bushrod leads us, maybe go back to the hotel and sleep the rest of the day. I'm tired, men are chasing us for God knows what, and now I've met a cool guy and he's already ditching me."

Seth leaned forward and put his hands on her shoulders. "I'm not ditching you. But you just said everything I was thinking. I'm tired too. Why are these men chasing us? What information do we have that they don't?"

They stared at each other for a few moments and Seth cocked his head and looked away. "They're never going to leave us alone, Madison."

She gazed at him with wrinkled eyebrows. "What do you mean? We gave them the book."

"Yeah, but listen," Seth pleaded, "we took the clue from the Ross steps. Even if they find the staircase in the Kent museum, the note Bushrod left is gone. That's why they're following us. They need us to find whatever it is they can't."

"What if we stop looking? What if we don't find it?" she asked.

He looked at her. "Then, they'll beat the shit out of us until we tell them what we know."

"Well I'm not tellin' them anything," she said.

"Me neither," Seth concurred. His cell phone rang in his pocket. Harper's Grove. He answered, "Hey Granddad."

"Where the hell you been?"

"At Valley Forge Park for some time now, sorry, didn't realize the time."

"What'd ya find?" Arthur asked.

"Listen, we're going back to the hotel or the library maybe. I'll call ya later." He hung up before he got a response. He took one last look around the parking lot and didn't see anything out of the ordinary. "Looks like you really did lose them. Let's get to a library and find out all we can about this Bushrod guy."

CHAPTER 16

The Montgomery County Library was the closest one to the park, according to the GPS in her car. They found it and went inside. Seth scanned the parking lot once again but didn't see anything unusual. The days of finding books using old-fashioned card catalogs were over. They saw at least a dozen small computer stations throughout the sprawling complex, not including eight additional ones that were used for Internet access. Madison walked over to the first one and typed in "Bushrod Washington". Only four books appeared on the screen and two were over at another library. She found the call numbers and they memorized each one.

Seth looked up and down at the numbers and letters on the ends of each aisle until he found the non-fiction section. They walked down two aisles, found the correct book and pulled it out of its place. It was thin, only a hundred eighty pages authored by a man named Kent Janikowski. It was entitled *The Washington*

Family Tree.

Seth flipped open the book and read the table of contents until he came to chapter nine, 'Washington's Nieces and Nephews'. He turned to the page number and Bushrod was listed first, alphabetically.

"Bushrod Washington was a U.S. Supreme Court Associate Justice and nephew of George Washington," Seth began. He finished the quick biography of Washington, skimming the paragraphs.

"Damn, nothing useful here," Seth said. "Let's try the other book." They put the book away and went down another aisle until Madison found the book they were looking for on the bottom shelf: *Washington's Final Years* by Frank Gorro. This, too, was divided into chapters, but there was no mention of nephews. Confused, Madison flipped to the index at the back of the book and looked for Bushrod's name. There it was. Mentioned on pages 34-35 and 89-92. She started on page thirty-four.

They read for a few moments, turning to page thirty-five but still found nothing of significance. Madison turned to page eighty-nine and this time read aloud to Seth:

"In his dying days Washington was sick with pneumonia and succumbed quickly. He was tended to by Martha and others that worked in the house. The one person that was there on the day he died was Bushrod Washington, his nephew. This is when it is reasoned, that George Washington changed his will and left part of his inheritance to Bushrod. Washington had some money; he was a soldier and the First President of The United States of America. What he did have to give to

Bushrod though, was a nice piece of property on the edge of the Potomac River, Mount Vernon."

She stopped reading and looked at Seth. "Bingo."

"Let's go." She closed the book, put it back in its place and they both moved toward the exit, and that's when they noticed Kohler outside the glass doors, smiling.

Seth looked for another exit but couldn't find one, so they turned back to Kohler. Nothing would happen here, it was a public library. He grabbed Madison's hand and they walked out the door.

"Where's Costello?" Seth asked, stopping short of Kohler.

He ignored the question. "Any good books you recommend?"

A thought occurred to Seth and he asked, "How'd you find us?"

Kohler ignored the question again. "Lemme tell you something, Seth. Those three Brits that stumbled upon your girlfriend's house last night? You don't want to piss them off. Me, I'm a reasonable man, but I can't vouch for those three."

"Who are they?" Madison asked.

"Beats the hell out of me. I just met them last night too. I would just be careful. Why don't we go somewhere and talk. I can protect you."

"Protect me from what?" Seth asked.

"I don't know, but wouldn't you feel better if we talked? I can assure you they would never find you."

"Am I under arrest?" Seth asked defiantly.

Kohler held up his hands, "Whoa, I'm no cop, Seth."

"Then leave us the hell alone." He grabbed Madison's hand and they walked down the steps to their car. They looked around and saw Costello leaning against a car smoking a cigarette. *Damn, how had they found us?* His cell phone buzzed in his pocket and he read the caller ID, Harper's Grove. He pushed the ignore button and they got in the car.

"Head to Harper's Grove," he told Madison.

She looked at him as she turned the ignition, "You sure you wanna bring him?"

"No, but he'll love every minute of it."

Maximus had a great rest in Madison's bed. He thought of her sleeping there every night and breathed in her femininity. He pictured her coming out of the shower, tossing the towel on the floor, grabbing *REDBOOK* from her nightstand and sliding into bed naked. He put his hands behind his head and interlocked his fingers. He thought of the other suckers out there taking turns watching the house, Evan then Chloe, Evan then Chloe. He didn't bother to split up and watch Seth's house even though he told the Americans he would. He had it under control.

Maximus peeked out the bedroom door and saw Evan on the recliner and Chloe on the couch, both sound asleep. He closed the door, stepped into the bathroom and turned on the shower. Before hopping in, he called Bannister in London and briefed him on last night's events.

"So, what's the book say?" Bannister asked.

"There's not much there, honestly. It lists Washington's relatives, and then some connect the dots sort of puzzle that no one could figure out."

"Have you heard from the Americans today?"

"Not yet, but we will."

"Bloody hell," Bannister shouted. "Let me get Castle on the line. I want you blokes ready to go as soon as I call you back."

Max tried to end the call before his boss did but Bannister beat him to the punch. He undressed and took a long hot shower. He thought about Madison but thought even more about Chloe sleeping on the couch. Chloe came into the group four months earlier, and according to her records, she was a criminal. That was no surprise, they were all criminals, but Chloe was different. She led small groups of women into Northern Ireland and carried out small, but important tasks, completely on her own.

The first one was a bank robbery. It was the largest bank in Belfast. After they killed two guards and blew the door off the safe, they made their getaway underground in the sewer, crippling the region by making off with over eight million Euros. The next task was setting fire to an important politician's home. After that, she blew up a private airplane carrying five IRA extremists on vacation. The British Intelligence Agency knew all along who she was and what she was doing, but they let her get away with it. They kept her in check, but also fed her information. Bannister recruited her specifically to work with Max. They were a good team.

Max toweled off in the bedroom. Chloe knocked

on the door and walked through. She yawned once before saying, “What’s the plan?”

“Damn,” Max said, wrapping the towel around him. “If I knew you were up, I would’ve waited to shower.”

“Piss off, Max.”

His cell rang again. It was Bannister.

“Yeah?”

“I just got off the phone with Castle. His men tracked them to Valley Forge Park and then to some library nearby. He doesn’t know where they’re going, but he has a tracker on them. They just picked up the old man and are heading south on Interstate 95.”

“Got it,” Max said.

“So get the hell in your car and start heading south. I’ll keep you posted whenever I hear something.”

Max ended the call and looked at Chloe. “Let’s get moving.”

“Where?”

“South,” he responded.

“DC?”

“That’s my guess.” Max said. He watched her leave and quickly dressed. All three of them were out the door within ten minutes, stopping only once for coffee before picking up the exit to I-95 South.

Chapter 17

By the time they got Arthur at Harper's Grove, signed the forms and convinced the woman at the desk that Arthur would not be gone for too long, it was nearing twelve noon. This was past Arthur's lunch hour. He was used to eating breakfast at seven, lunch at eleven-thirty, and dinner at four-thirty. Most nights he was in bed by eight-thirty. It wasn't more than fifteen minutes into the trip that Arthur complained every other minute that he was hungry. Madison drove, Seth rode shotgun and Arthur sat in back.

After being on I-95 for only a few minutes they entered the state of Delaware. Two exits down, Seth told Madison to turn off and make a right at the bottom of the exit. They traveled only two miles with Seth directing until they turned right again and pulled into a small strip mall of shops. Close to the end was Capriotti's Sandwich Shop. They parked, got out of the car and went in.

Seth told them all about Capriotti's sandwiches before they arrived and they knew what to order when they walked in. It was not a sit down place, just a counter and a kitchen. Seth ordered a cheese-steak with mushrooms, Madison ordered a turkey hoagie and Arthur got the turkey special, called a "Bobbie." It was a turkey hoagie on a long roll with stuffing and cranberry sauce. Arthur salivated as Seth described it to him.

After ten minutes, Seth paid for the sandwiches and a couple of iced teas and they were back in their car heading south. Arthur inhaled his sandwich.

"Don't get any on my seats!" Madison said.

Seth held her hoagie in one hand and ate his steak with the other.

"Man, this is good," Arthur said between bites.

"Granddad," Seth said quietly, "we wanna hear the truth."

"What truth?" Arthur responded.

"How'd you get the book—Washington's book?"

Arthur stopped mid-chew and looked up at Seth who was half-turned in the front seat. He dabbed a napkin all over his mouth and cheeks and finished chewing before responding. "I stole it," he said.

Madison and Seth stopped mid-bite.

"From whom?" Seth said.

"Listen Seth, I hope you don't think any less of me for doing so, but I was in no position to do what was right."

"What do you mean Granddad?"

"Remember your dad telling you I traveled all over the place because I was in the military? Well, that wasn't the whole truth."

Seth nodded. "I'm listening."

"I was chasing this book, Seth. I just didn't know where it was. I first learned about it in the Marines. I was stationed on a small island outside Korea and became good friends with a fellow named Willie Wright, Dub-Dub we called him after his initials." He rolled up the papers the sandwich came in and passed the trash to Seth who took it and put it in the brown paper bag. "One night, we stole some liquor from the chief and went down to the beach and started drinking it. Man we got drunk. We hadn't had a drink in over two months so we had a good ol' time. Anyways, Dub-Dub started tellin' me about these crazy stories that he was related to someone who was related to someone else who was related to George Washington."

"Really," Madison said in disbelief. "Your Marine buddy was related to Washington?"

"Yeah, I didn't know if it was the whiskey talking or what, but he went on and on so I let him talk. Next thing I know, he tells me about a diary or journal of Washington's that is in his family's possession."

"Our book," Seth said.

"Yeah, our book. I still can't believe you gave it to those limey bastards," Arthur said.

Seth started to say something in protest but Arthur held up his hand. "So I started asking him what was in the book and who had it but he didn't know. He just said it was important because they moved it from family to family so no one had it very long. He said it was passed down five or six generations."

"Did he say anything about Bushrod?" Seth asked.

"Not that I recall. I would've remembered a name like that."

"So what'd you do?" Madison asked.

"Well, we got shipped back to the states six months later but he never brought it up again. Frankly, after we got back here, I never saw him again. Well, I did see him once."

"When?"

"The night I took the book," he said.

"You stole it from your Marine buddy?" Seth asked.

"You gotta understand, son. Coming back to the states, we had nothing. I had no job, your grandma was pregnant with your dad's sister, we were broke. I thought, hey, if that book was valuable, I could have sold it for some money."

Seth looked up at the toll booth and they glided through with the cars' EZ-Pass tag. A few moments later they saw a sign that said Welcome to Maryland.

"Then what?" Seth asked reluctantly.

"Well, I tracked Dub-Dub down and found out he was living in a suburb of Baltimore, so I paid him a visit. I called him on the phone; we chatted for almost an hour about our time in the Corps. He said he wasn't married at the time and had no kids. I drove down there from our home in Philly then called him and asked him to meet me for lunch. I showed up all right, but I was late."

"Why?" asked Madison.

"Well, I knew he was out of his house and that's when I broke in and took the book."

Seth started to say something but Arthur

interrupted. "I'm not proud of what I did Seth. I'm ashamed of it till this day. I was a different person back then."

"How'd you know he had the book?"

"I searched everywhere. I knew his mother had it and I even paid her a visit one time asking her about the book. She sniffed me out and I left without it. Then, Dub-Dub's mom died and I waited until things settled down and thought that this was my chance."

"How'd you know where to look?" Madison asked.

Arthur chuckled. "Dub-Dub was obsessed with fishing. That's all he talked about when we were stationed on this small island. He even rigged up a homemade fishing rod and was catching little fish right there on the beach. Well, when we got to talking on the phone, he told me about a trip he took out of the Florida Keys a few years back. He said he hooked into a monster tarpon that took him three hours to pull in. Can you imagine that?"

Seth and Madison stared out at the long stretch of highway in front of them and waited for Arthur to finish his story.

"He told me he had it stuffed and mounted and it was sitting on a wall in his office at home. I knew right then, that's where he would put the book, inside the tarpon. Dub-Dub was a simple guy and he wouldn't go to all the trouble of a security box at a bank or a safe in his house. So, when he was out at the restaurant waiting for me, I broke in the back door and found the book in no time, right there inside the big fish."

"Wow," Seth said. "Did you go to the restaurant?"

"Oh yeah, I was only a few minutes late. At the

time, I acted like everything was normal. I was even giddy with excitement. Then, after a few weeks and I couldn't figure out any of the puzzles or clues, I gave up. I bought the safety deposit box, hid the key and forgot about it."

"That's some story, Arthur. Is Dub-Dub still alive?"

"Beats me," he said. "That was the last I ever talked to him or saw him. I thought about giving it back but I just couldn't bring myself to do it." Arthur leaned against the window in the back seat and stared at the empty fields. They were through the Baltimore tunnel and less than an hour away from Mount Vernon.

Secret Service Agents Kohler and Pierce trailed about five miles behind Madison. Kohler was driving and Pierce had his laptop out plugged into the cigarette lighter to keep it charged. He had a wireless card in the USB slot that gave him constant internet connection during their trip. He was using a software package that allowed them to trace the car's route down to the tenth of a mile. This was something not available to the general public, strictly government use. Every now and then, he would change websites and look at ESPN.com. That is, until Kohler would catch him and he got back to trailing them.

"How's a screw-up like you end up in security detail for the VP?" Kohler asked.

"I take offense to that," Pierce responded.

"I call them like I see 'em, Pierce. You're

overweight, you've only been an agent seven years, and you're a hothead."

"Well, this time, I won't argue with those points. Between you and me," he lowered his voice, "my dad was in the same fraternity as Castle. Skull & Bones, ever hear of it?"

"Shit yeah, the Bush's were in that up at Yale. All these political guys were in that fraternity. Same time?"

"Nah, Castle has five years on my dad. But, he called in a little favor and here I am."

"Aren't *I* lucky."

"How about you? You've been doing this eighteen years. How come you don't have the big guy as your detail?" Pierce asked.

Kohler thought for a moment before responding. He didn't need to tell his partner anything but he did anyway. "I'll never get the POTUS detail. About ten years ago, I had security detail for him when he was first running in the primary as Governor of New Jersey. As you know, everyone that has at least a shot at becoming president gets security detail from the Secret Service."

"Course," Pierce chimed in, like he knew everything.

"Well, here I am guarding this guy on his campaign trail, which he obviously lost, and we're stuck in a massive snow storm in Newark. Well, he pulls me into his hotel room and…"

"And what?"

"He asks me to get him a hooker," Kohler said.

Pierce laughed out loud. "That's great, what'd you say?"

"I told him I wouldn't do it."

"Damn, really?"

"Yeah, man. Here this guy is, running for the office of President and he wants a hooker during his layover."

"That took some balls."

Kohler nodded. "Maybe I should have, I don't know. Maybe I'd be his right hand man during his Presidency."

"Yeah, but you could've blackmailed him. You could've insisted you get on his detail."

"Believe me," Kohler said, eyes straight ahead on the road, "he asked me to be on his detail the week after he got elected. He almost begged me, knowing I could ruin him. But I resisted. I didn't wanna work for a prick like that."

"Instead," Pierce laughed again, "you're working for a prick like Castle."

"They're all pricks, Pierce. Every last one of them."

They drove in silence for a while until Castle called him asking for an update. They said they just crossed into Virginia and were making their way on the Beltway, about three miles behind the car. The traffic was light, which was surprising for DC. They knew in less than an hour it would be bumper to bumper as everyone made their way home. Kohler still couldn't figure out where the car was going. Maybe they were running. Just driving south for Florida? That all changed a few miles later when they pulled off an exit that said, "Mount Vernon".

CHAPTER 18

Large aircraft flew in low from the east as they parked their car in the visitor's lot. The roar was loud enough, in certain cases, to cause most people to look up into the sky as the military aircraft made their way to nearby Davison Airport at Fort Belvoir. Ever since 9/11, people had their guard up whenever a plane could be seen or heard at such an altitude. Fortunately, nothing like that atrocity had happened again. Seth looked up and saw a large C-130, bank ever so slightly north, and continue its decent toward touchdown.

The parking lot at Mount Vernon was almost full with cars showcasing license plates from all over the east coast. Maryland, Delaware, New Jersey, Pennsylvania, Virginia, DC, even one from Georgia. Yellow school buses parked neatly in a row towards the back of the lot, their cluster taking over one third of the available spaces. Seth and Madison got out of their car as Arthur snored softly in the backseat.

"Should we wake him?" Madison asked.

Seth shook his head and said, "Nah, let him sleep. Lock the doors, crack the windows and we'll come back and get him."

She pushed the button on her keychain and the headlights blinked twice in recognition. They looked around and saw people walking around in small groups. They followed them to the admission gate, bought their tickets and walked through a building and out the other side onto the Mount Vernon plantation. They followed a path with an eight foot high stone wall on their left that enclosed a few sheep, and gardens on their right. As they came around the wall, they could see the house that was called Mount Vernon. Some people stopped to take pictures; others just gazed at the large house on the top of the hill. There were a few different buildings that comprised Mount Vernon. The largest was obviously the house, the others were smaller, a few barns, an outhouse, etc. They talked it over in the car and realized they had no idea where to look, so they started walking up the stone walkway toward the house.

It was a mansion by any respect—three stories tall, but wide with large white pillars that separated the porch from the second floor. Two chimneys towered on either end of the house and a glass enclosure stood in the middle of the roof, looking almost like a lighthouse. They got in line to enter the house and were soon handed a brochure from a young woman at the front door.

They first walked through the slave quarters which were small and then proceeded to enter the house through the back door. They stood in the downstairs foyer with about eight other people, all starting the tour. An elderly woman stood there and waited until the door closed before she spoke. "Welcome to Mount Vernon, home of our Founding Father, George Washington," she began. "Feel free to look into the rooms on either side."

The rooms were blocked with velvet ropes so that you could not enter them but Seth and Madison peeked into the rooms, one by one, while the woman continued talking. All of the rooms were small and the first one on the right had a tiny piano in it as well as a small eating table. Past that was another dining room and across the hall a third eating area. The first room on the left had a small bed in it and all four rooms had fireplaces.

"One of the first things George Washington did was double the width of the staircase. As you walk up the stairs, feel free to touch the railing and imagine who might have touched this railing before you."

As they walked up the stairs, Seth put his hand on the railing and looked up at the ornate plaster designs on the ceiling. They reached the second floor and a chubby fellow stood at attention waiting for everyone to arrive.

"Here you have five of the nine bedrooms in the house. Another three are located upstairs. At one point, six-hundred guests stayed here over the course of a year, so you can imagine the need for all the rooms."

The landing was small and they weren't allowed to step into any of the rooms which frustrated Seth and kept him from looking at anything of importance.

"The crib you see here was for Martha's grandchild who stayed in this room," the man said. "If you continue along the hallway you will see the private wing that George had built in 1774."

They followed the group of people and stopped outside of another bedroom where they were greeted by an elderly woman.

"This is the private bedroom of George and Martha Washington," she began.

Madison peered in and whispered to Seth," Pretty cool, eh?" It was much larger than the other bedrooms and featured two walk-in closets in the back. A teenaged boy to her right pulled out his smart phone and aimed it at the bed.

"Please, no pictures!" the woman said abruptly.

"Although it doesn't look like it, this bed is actually the largest in the house at six and a half feet in length. This was to accommodate George's six foot two height. This is also the bedroom where George died with Martha by his side. As was custom in the day, she moved immediately from this room to a bedroom on the third floor. Ninety percent of what you see here has been untouched in over two-hundred years."

Seth and Madison took their time looking around. It had a seating area and a walk-in closet, unlike the other bedrooms. They followed the group back to the first floor where they saw Washington's office. Another gentleman told them about the four desks in the room and the large glass bookshelves. On their way outside, they passed a small kitchen.

"Seth, there's no way we're going to find anything here. We don't even know where to look, and besides there are guards everywhere," Madison pleaded.

He looked around, trying to decide what to do.

They could check out the other buildings, but he didn't even know what they were looking for yet. Something kept drawing his eye back to the path they had come up. He pointed his finger. "Let's walk over there."

They walked the same path and turned left down a steep hill. Cows grazed to their right and they turned left at the dirt turnoff and followed the walkway to a red brick one story-building with an American flag out front. Two large obelisks stood outside the tomb of the first president.

"On the right is George Washington and on the left is his wife Martha," said a voice from behind. They turned and saw a tall, elderly black man standing behind them with his hands behind his back. He was dressed in the security detail that they saw at the front gates.

"How'd they die?" Seth asked.

"Oh, natural causes. Back in the early eighteen hundreds if you were ill, chances are you succumbed to pneumonia."

"Is it true that Bushrod Washington inherited Mount Vernon?" Seth asked.

"Sure is," the man responded. "Homes and plantations were passed around a lot in those days. People died and it was passed to the next generation. Why the interest in Bushrod?"

Seth and Madison just looked at each other, not knowing how to respond. "Just curious, I guess," Seth said.

The man looked at them. "You look familiar, ever been here before?"

Seth shook his head and before he could respond, another voice came from the entryway, this time more familiar.

"There you are!" It was Arthur, walking toward them. "I've been looking all over for you. How dare you leave an old man in the car with those maniacs out there!"

The older black man turned and stared at the man that just walked into the open-air tomb. He locked eyes with the new guest and his mouth opened wide. "Arthur," he managed to say.

Arthur stared back in disbelief and said, "Dub-Dub."

Updates were pouring into the cell phone of Vice-President Castle. His assistant/mistress walked in and even she got nudged away. The first report came in that Kohler and Pierce followed them to Mount Vernon, the site of George Washington's house and burial site. His men didn't follow them in the house, just waited outside in the parking lot. All the while, Bannister was calling from London so that he could update his team.

Castle considered lying to Bannister. He didn't want a full scale shoot-out on the grounds of a National Landmark. In the end, he updated Bannister who in turn updated Max, Evan and Chloe, who were about twenty minutes behind his security detail. Kohler had called again, upset that the Brits were there too, but Castle ignored him and told him to finish the job. He didn't give a damn who found the document.

CHAPTER 19

The sun dove into the west, darkening the tomb. A chill filled the air as the two men stared at each other for a few moments and recognition set in. One, a black man, was staring at his former Marine buddy from thirty years ago. The other, the man who had stolen his family heirloom, was staring right back. Arthur felt some type of embarrassment. Did Dub-Dub know that he had taken the book? He decided not to broach the subject and instead, walked slowly forward, extending his right hand. The other man did the same. Soon they fully embraced and smiles engulfed their faces.

"Damn, I haven't heard that nickname in twenty years. Last reunion I guess. I go by Willie now. Speaking of the reunion, where the hell were you?"

"Ah shucks, you know me," Arthur responded. "I don't much care to reminisce about the war. Hell, we lost a lot of good men."

"Damn right we did." He turned to face Seth and

Madison. "Your grandkids, Walt?"

"Just the boy, and that's his girlfriend."

Neither Seth nor Madison objected to the term. They still couldn't believe what they were seeing.

"So what are you doing here?" Willie asked.

No one answered for a split second and Willie raised his eyebrows before Arthur spoke.

"Just showing them around some historic sites, you know? What's more famous than Mount Vernon, eh, Dub, I mean Willie?"

Willie turned back to Arthur then swiveled his head over to Seth and Madison. "The hell you are," he said. "All this interest about Bushrod Washington, now I know. Who the hell knew about Bushrod anyway? Not unless you are some history buff, which I know you're not. But, it was in Washington's journal in capital letters, wasn't it Arthur?"

The blood drained from Arthur's face, and Willie jumped all over it.

"You stole my book you son of a bitch!" He walked two steps and got right in Arthur's face. "All these years I couldn't figure it out. My house was never burglarized; I never got crazy phone calls or was followed. But you, you came down here, what twenty-five years ago and were late to that lunch that you arranged. You broke in and stole it, didn't you?"

Arthur turned and saw a group of people approach. Willie didn't want anyone to hear their discussion so he walked away in the opposite direction. They followed Willie down the stone path that opened up into a large circular area with what appeared to be a memorial of some sorts in the middle. Willie stopped and paused.

He bowed his head for several seconds as if in reverence. Seth and Madison looked at each other and shrugged their shoulders. They were curious enough to walk into the center of the memorial and this time Seth read aloud, "In memory of the Afro Americans who served as slaves at Mount Vernon. This monument marking their burial ground dedicated September 21, 1983. Mount Vernon Ladies Association."

"Didn't you?" Willie asked again. He lowered his voice and stepped away. "Your lack of an answer is proof enough." He put his hand to his head and exhaled. "Can never trust anyone, can you? Man, Arthur, we were good buds in the Corps; I never thought you'd do something like this."

"I'm sorry," was all Arthur could muster.

They looked out through the trees at the Potomac River, a wide expanse of water that stretched all the way south to the Atlantic Ocean.

Willie swiped his hand through the air. "What's the difference now anyway? I'm too old to care about something so long ago. But, I wanted to hand that down to my daughter. You still have it?"

"I'm sorry," Arthur said again.

Seth spoke up, "I lost it, sir."

"No you didn't," Arthur said, defending his grandson.

"Yes, Granddad, I did. Well, technically, I didn't lose it, I gave it away."

"What?" Willie exclaimed.

"You see sir, we were being chased and—"

"Willie, you got a place we can talk?" Arthur asked.

He scanned the faces of all three people before responding. He was older, yes, wiser, yes, but the kindness never left him. "My shift is over in fifteen minutes. We can go to my house only a few miles from here."

They started walking towards the exit when Arthur stopped Willie and apologized once more. Willie just stared into the empty eyes and shook his head.

"Mind if I ride with ya?" Arthur asked.

Willie thought for moment, rolled his eyes, and nodded toward the exit.

"Here we go, mates," Max said to the other four people. The Brits had met up with the Secret Service agents and they had hunkered down at a picnic table near a small food cart on the grounds of Mount Vernon. The guys had gotten hot dogs and Coke's, and Chloe had a soft pretzel and bottled water. Surprisingly, they were getting along, for now. All five heads turned in the direction Max was looking and saw the three people they were chasing walking down the hill towards the parking lot. They were being led by a tall skinny black man.

"Who's the stiff?" Evan asked.

"Beats me," answered Kohler. He scrunched up his hot dog wrapper and downed the last bite. While they sat there killing time Kohler said, "So, you guys government, SIS, MI6, Interpol?"

"Maybe they're Scotland Yard," Pierce joked.

"Funny, fatso," Chloe announced, causing murmurs

of laughter around the table. "You don't wanna know what we are."

"'Cause then you'd have to kill us, right?" Kohler said, humoring her.

"We could kill ya anyway," Chloe responded, "for being so incompetent that I had to fly across the Atlantic to handle two pips and their old man."

Pierce defended himself. "Incompetent my ass. We had the job in hand. We don't need you limey bastards."

"Who you callin' limey?" Evan said.

"You, tough guy," Pierce responded, getting up from his chair. Evan got up as well and started walking around the table.

"Sit the hell down, the both of you," Kohler said. "Settle this later." He watched the two men stare at each other and slowly return to their seats.

Kohler and Max watched the two of them get in their car and follow the two in the white pick-up truck out of the lot. They all waited in silence, the tension building between the five of them until the car was out of sight.

"Time to roll," Kohler said.

"Try and keep up," Pierce said to Evan.

Evan flipped him the finger and the groups separated and got into their own cars, following the two vehicles ahead.

CHAPTER 20

The town of Belle Haven was middle class to say the least. A lot of brownstones lined the street on both sides with thin trees jutting out of the brick sidewalks. They followed Willie in his truck and parked outside of his house.

"Guess they talked it out," Seth said, nodding to Willie and Arthur as they made their way out of the car, joking and laughing. They followed Willie up the front steps and through the front door and into his home. Hardwood floors greeted them, and Seth stamped his feet on the throw rug like he had rain or snow on his shoes. They took off their light jackets and hung them on hooks near the front door. Willie walked down the short hallway toward the kitchen.

"I must be the most forgiving son of a bitch out there," Willie said.

"Yes, you are," Arthur replied, "and I thank you."

"Well, at my age, it does you no good to hold a

grudge after all this time. What are we drinkin?" he asked.

Arthur smacked his hands together and rubbed them briskly like he was making a fire. "Whatcha got?"

Willie looked him over. "I got something for you." He reached under the counter and brought out a dark green bottle with no label on it. "Made this myself."

"What is it?" Arthur asked.

"Let's just call it whiskey for now," Willie responded.

He grabbed two small glasses from the cabinet and poured three fingers worth of a brown liquid. "How about you two?" he asked.

"No thanks," Madison said, turning her nose up.

"I'm good," Seth replied.

Willie reached into the refrigerator, pulled out two bottles of water and handed one to each of his guests. He grabbed one of the glasses of liquor, handed it to Arthur and then grabbed the other one for himself.

"I would recite the Corps motto but I think I forgot it." He raised his glass, tilted it to Arthur who did the same and said, "To old friends and to new friends."

"Semper Fi," Arthur said.

They touched glasses and both men downed the drink in one gulp.

Arthur's face twisted and he closed his eyes. "That's terrible!" he said.

"Ahh, you'll get used to it," Willie responded, pouring another shot for both of them. "Let's go in the den," Willie said to Seth, "your granddad tells me you have one hell of a story."

They entered the small room with framed pictures

covering the walls. Most were of a young woman. The ages were progressive through the years of her life. There were a few pictures of an infant, then as a young girl, a teenager, and how she looked at present. There were also three pictures of another woman, older than the first.

"That there is Rebecca, my daughter."

"I thought you never married," Arthur said.

"That was years ago. I *was* married and we had Rebecca."

"Was? You divorced?"

Willie paused for a moment. "Rebecca's mother died on 9/11. She worked at the Pentagon. Rebecca was only ten years old at the time."

Madison put her hand to her mouth and said, "Oh, I'm so sorry."

Willie sat in one of the fabric chairs and Arthur sat next to him. A small table was between them where they rested their drinks. "Ahh, don't worry about it. That was years ago. I'll never get over it but I've learned to live with it. Without Rebecca, I don't know where I'd be today."

Madison and Seth sat down on the brown leather couch opposite the chairs.

"So," Willie said, quickly changing the subject. "What's so important you have to tell me?"

"I'll start," Seth said. He told the story beginning with him finding the key in his granddad's attic and ended with them showing up at Mount Vernon that day.

"So that's why we were at the tomb today."

"You think it's here?" Willie asked.

Seth turned his hands over and gave a slight shake

of his head. "I have no other reason to search anywhere else. If he moved it from the Ross house, then again from Valley Forge, it must be at Mount Vernon. His uncle gave him the property and he lived there until he died, right?"

"That he did," Willie said, leaning back in the chair, in deep thought.

"The problem is," Seth added, "where in the world do we look? And how?"

Willie crossed his legs and took another sip of his drink. "I mean, it could be in the house, but," he shook his head, "there were so many people in that house back then, it would've probably been discovered. Plus, it's been renovated, gutted, painted over; all kinds of new things have been put in to replace the old stuff. If he put it in that house, it's probably gone or hidden somewhere really good."

"What about the tombs?" Madison asked suddenly.

Willie looked at her. I hope you're not suggesting we dig up his grave?"

"I don't know what I'm suggesting," Madison pleaded, "I'm just saying that tombs and graves and coffins don't go through a renovation process. They put a body in; they never take it out or change the surroundings."

"True," Willie said, leaning back in chair again, eyes gazing on the ceiling.

"Bushrod's buried there, correct?"

"Yep, along with a lot of other Washington family members."

"Hey," Arthur said, "how'd you get this job of yours anyway? What are you doing there?"

Willie answered proudly, "I am a security guard there. After the Corps, I worked security for a bunch of outfits. I moved to DC with my wife after she got a job at the Pentagon and I took a job for a big law firm. Retired six years ago and was really bored sitting around all day. So, I work there three days a week."

"I also hear that you are related to George Washington," Seth noted, breaking the silence.

Willie didn't answer right away but looked directly at Arthur. "That's for another discussion," he said softly.

"So how about you take us back to Vernon tonight?" Arthur asked.

Willie turned in his chair to face Arthur and put his hands on his knees. "Are you outta your mind? That's a National Landmark we're talking about, Arthur. You can't just go traipsing around in the middle of the night. I'd get fired for one and we'd all be arrested!"

"Yeah, Granddad, we can't ask him to do that."

Arthur looked around the room, took one last sip of his drink and put the glass down loudly on the table. "Let's go home then. I'm tired, and if you are all just gonna give up then let's forget it. This book has been around for over two hundred years. You two traveled all over Philly to find these clues and now you drove three hours to give up? Fine, let's go."

Madison was the first to speak. "Arthur, wait. Willie, I have an idea."

Willie started to open his mouth in protest but Madison spoke first.

"What if we all went there, and if something happens and we get caught, you're the hero who caught us. You stay dressed in your uniform, and if the cops or anyone else see us, you say you caught us after hours snooping around."

"What is my reason for being there at such an hour?" Willie asked.

She shrugged her shoulders and said, "Just make something up. You left your phone there and went to pick it up. You were out to dinner and just happened to drive by and see us. They won't care why you were there."

"What if you turn on me and say it was all my idea?" Willie asked.

Arthur leaned in. "Dub-Dub, it's me were talking about here. I would never do such a thing."

"And you're going to take full responsibility on this? The three of you?"

Madison looked at Seth who nodded then looked at Arthur who did the same.

Willie let out an exaggerated sigh. He stood up, picked up his drink and said, "Let's get something to eat. We leave at nine o'clock,"

Arthur smacked his hands together and exclaimed, "Hot damn!"

CHAPTER 21

It looked like the ghosts chasing Pac-man as the four cars made their way back to Mount Vernon. Arthur rode shotgun in Willie's truck, followed by Seth and Madison in her car, then a mile back were the Feds in the SUV and the Brits in a rented sedan. There was not much traffic on the George Washington Memorial Parkway, so the first two cars were well clear of the second set of cars as they made their way along the winding road that hugged the Potomac River.

It was dark on the river, too early in the season to have boats out, or more likely the yachts. Seth and Madison followed Willie toward their destination just a few minutes away. They bought three flashlights with batteries, a crowbar, two cigarette lighters, a shovel, three keychain vials of mace and a thirty foot piece of rope at the hardware store. They had no idea what they'd use them for, but one never knew what to bring when exploring gravesites.

Willie's truck pulled off the main road and followed the signs to their destination. He'd never been there so late. They pulled up to the now closed Mount Vernon. Two iron gates spanned the length of both sides of the road in a triangle configuration. Willie positioned his car in the middle of the gate, and pointed his headlights at the padlock that secured both sides. He turned the ignition off, grabbed his keys and exited the truck without saying a word. Willie made his way to the padlock, gave a quick glance around and unlocked the gate. The lock came open with a snap and he pushed the gate to the edge of the grass, giving the cars enough room to pass. He got back in the truck, started the car and led the way in. He parked close to the back of the parking lot, opened his window, and with a wave of his hand, directed Madison to park further away so it appeared they were not together.

The cars were turned off, headlights doused, and the four of them exited their vehicles and met near the edge of the lot. It was dark, but there were a half a dozen spotlights positioned on twenty-foot poles in the parking lot so they were not in complete darkness. They looked up at the mansion. Two lonely porch lights were on in the back and a couple windows on the first floor had light coming from them.

"Are you sure no one is here?" Seth asked.

"No," Willie replied, "but I think there's a good chance the place is empty. There are no cars here and there's no one that lives here. It's for visitors only."

"Then let's get moving. I wanna start at the tombs."

They walked up the stone pathway that interweaved

all of the buildings on the grounds of Mount Vernon. As they reached the tomb, almost instinctively, they all turned to look up at the mansion to make sure they were alone. So far, they were. Tiny little spotlights were lit in the ground illuminating the area designated for Washington's tomb.

They approached the black wrought iron gates which were locked with a padlock. To the right and left of the gates were the tall white obelisks. They looked like miniature versions of the Washington Monument in DC. They too, were enclosed inside a black iron fence, but Seth brought his flashlight out and shined it on the one to the left and read aloud, "In memory of John Augustine Washington and his wife Eleanor Love Senden. Who's that?"

Willie spoke up, "He was the great grand-nephew of George, a famous Confederate army officer. He was the last Washington to technically own Mount Vernon."

Madison walked around to the right obelisk and read from the large column, "Within the vault lies buried the immortal remains of Bushrod Washington, an associate justice of the Supreme Court of the U.S. He died in Philadelphia November 26th, 1829, aged 68. By his side is interred his devoted wife, Anna Blackburn, who survived her beloved husband but two days, aged sixty."

Between the two towers was a small path that led to the actual tombs. There was an open archway made of brick. Seth shone his flashlight on the top of the opening and read, "Within this enclosure rest the remains of General George Washington." The gates that encompassed him were locked. He shone his flashlight inside and they could make out two caskets of what appeared to be brushed white concrete or maybe even marble. They were very smooth with ornate designs on the top.

"Those two tombs are for George and Martha, not what you're looking for. Follow me, we can't get in this way," Willie said. He led them to the right of the vault, around to the side. Willie searched through his vast amount of keys until he found the right one. "This here is a storage closet of some sort. I only use the broom inside to sweep dirt and leaves around the tomb." Before he inserted the key, he said, "I am not going in with you. You do not desecrate these graves, is that understood?"

All three of them nodded in agreement.

"I will be on the other side keeping watch. Once you enter this room, I will not be able to see you. It is a separate room from the tombs at the front. At the first sign of trouble, you get your asses out the back and away from here. I'll deny everything. I hope you will keep your end of the bargain. Deal?"

All three nodded—again.

Willie paused and said, "God forgive us all." He turned the key and opened the vault door.

It was tough for the Vice-President to sit in the Oval Office listening to the Secretary of State ramble on about some foreign affairs meeting she had with the Prime Minister of Egypt. Jon Castle had more important things on his mind. His phone had buzzed in his pocket twice in the past thirty minutes, and he couldn't bring himself to answer it in front of the President. He'd also blocked all text messaging to and from this phone; it was one less record of a conversation taking place. Castle had to wait until the meeting was over so he could make his call. His assistant, Kim, sat next to him on the couch and abruptly bumped his knee with hers, jarring him from his thoughts.

"Jon?" asked President Bowe again.

"Ah, yeah, I agree," Castle managed to say.

The President looked at him with cautious eyes. His tie was off and he was dressed in a canary oxford shirt and navy blue pants. His arms were crossed in front of his stout chest and his face flexed as he narrowed his eyes at Castle.

"Okay, then, it's settled. We agree to lend," he made imaginary quotation marks with his fingers, "the Egyptians two-hundred and fifty million US dollars for the right to place twelve F-15 fighters and an additional two thousand troops along the Egyptian-Libyan border."

"I think that's the right move, Mr. President," his Chief of Staff said, a thick man with a shaved head and a wrinkled nose.

"Good, anything else from the land of King Tut?" he asked his Secretary of State.

"That's it," she said.

Everyone got up to leave the Oval Office when the President said, "Jon, gimme a minute would you?"

The VP looked at him and spoke softly to Kim telling her to wait outside. He sat back down on the couch and watched as the President stayed leaning against the front of desk, arms still crossed.

"What's up, Jon?"

"Nothing much, sir, just a little tired I guess."

He unfolded his arms, stuck his hands in his pockets and casually walked over to the bookshelf in the near corner. He grabbed two bowl-shaped drinking glasses and reached into a miniature refrigerator below the shelf and pulled out what appeared to be a wine bottle. Bowe uncorked the bottle and poured into both glasses a fine white bubbly head that crested over a burnt orange liquid. He handed one to Castle and sat across from him in one of the chairs.

"This, Jon, is from a monastery on the outskirts of Belgium. Beer, Jon, not fancy scotch or bourbon or wine. Good old fashioned beer. Brewed by monks of all people. I was given a case by the head monk himself, don't even know his name. In fact, when I visited the monastery, I was going to buy some to take home. Whaddya know, huh?" He raised his glass and inched back in his chair. "The perks of being the President."

The two men took a swallow of beer and the President exhaled. "That is good stuff."

"Yes, sir," Castle agreed.

"So, you alright, Jon?"

"Never better, sir. Just tired like I said."

"Yeah, this job is tiring isn't it? But, Jon," the President leaned forward. "The job is not forever. Know what I mean?"

"Sure, all depends on the voters, right?"

"Sure does," the President agreed. Took another drink of his beer and watched Castle do the same. "You want my job, don't you, Jon?"

Castle was caught off guard and it showed in his face even though he tried to deny it. "What? No. I'm perfectly happy as VP."

"Sure, who wouldn't be, except the President, that is. Jon, you're perfectly welcome to seek my position again once it's that time. I figure we'll get re-elected for another term, then four years later, it's your turn."

"Sir, I am—"

The President put his hand up. "But in the meantime, I expect you to act like a VP and to take your job seriously—no drifting off in my meetings, no looking over at your assistant like you wanna bang her, which, well…I'll leave that alone. Get your head outta your ass and start being *my* Vice-President. Understood?"

"Yes sir," Castle said. He was embarrassed and quickly finished his drink.

"Good," the President said. He got out of his chair and Castle did the same. "Good talk, Jon." He slapped him on the back as they walked toward the door.

"Good beer too, sir," Castle said back to him, humoring him, placing his empty glass on the table.

"See you tomorrow."

Castle walked out the door and it was closed behind him. The guard outside nodded at him, and Castle walked down the hall until he saw Kim. He nudged her from behind and she followed him, past the Chief of Staff's office and turning the corner they went into his office and he closed the door.

"That son of a bitch," Castle said.

"Jon, keep your voice down," Kim said.

"I don't care. Who's gonna hear me anyway? Damn, that guy thinks he can walk all over me. If it wasn't for adding me to his ballot, he wouldn't even be in this position."

Kim wanted to say, *neither would you*, but she held back. She walked over to him and put her hands on his shoulders as he sat down at his desk. It was her turn to give the massage, but he was interrupted when his phone buzzed in his jacket pocket. He picked it up immediately.

"Where were you?" Kohler asked on the other line.

"Don't worry about it, what have you got?"

"We're outside the gates of Mount Vernon right now. They decided to sneak in after dark."

"Good, let them do whatever they want. Listen to your scanners, and if the police get a call about intruders, call it off."

"Gotcha, we'll take them as they leave."

"Good, keep me posted."

He hung up the phone and walked back to Kim who was looking at him with curious interest.

"Police?" she asked, "What's going on, Jon?"

"Don't worry about it, Kim." He smiled.

"It's my job to worry about you, Jon."

"That President of yours is going to have a lot more to worry about pretty soon."

Kim had a look of shock on her face.

"For now, my dear, let's worry about taking care of me." He grabbed her hand and led her over to the couch.

CHAPTER 22

The most recent public pictures at Washington's tomb were of George and Laura Bush. They'd gone there on February 19, 2007 to pay their respects to the man celebrating his 275th Birthday. Other than that, no one was allowed to take a picture. No one was allowed to enter the front of the tomb either, that's why Willie didn't have the keys, but he did have keys to the back storage closet. When he opened the door for them, Arthur quickly changed his mind and decided to stay outside with Willie. Seth and Madison entered the dark room with their flashlights off. The ground was sandy and gravelly. The crunch of their shoes echoed in the still darkness of the night.

Seth flicked his flashlight on and illuminated the floor, watching his careful steps as he made his way around the room. He stayed close to the walls at first with Madison trailing behind, flashlight off. He decided he needed to see more so he covered the flashlight lens with his hand and raised it waist-high. Seth slowly spread his fingers, bit by bit, allowing a little light to peak out, not knowing if this room had windows or not.

The walls were blank, just concrete blocks, but the floor wasn't. As he made his way around the edge of the dark room, he saw small slightly raised bronze plaques on the floor. They were about half the size of a piece of standard typewriter paper. They were fastened into the floor with screws in all four corners. The floor was dusty so neither he nor Madison could make out anything on them, but he could tell that there was text engraved on the face.

Madison flipped her flashlight on, knelt down on one knee and scanned her flashlight across the floor to reveal the numerous bronze plaques. She dusted the first plaque off and read aloud to Seth, "Augustine Washington 1694-1793." After she finished with that one, she crab-walked over to the next one, wiped her hand across it and read, "Mary Ball Washington 1708-1789."

Seth followed her lead, found a plaque at the top and read, "Anna Blackburn Washington, Bushrod's wife, we're close!" Seth moved to the next closest plaque, the one directly in the middle and dusted it off. It was Bushrod's.

"What now?" Madison asked?

Seth was caught off guard, *yes, what now*? He ran his fingers over the smooth plaque. There was no clasp or hook to lift it open. "Look around," he said.

Madison got up and shone her flashlight all around the room. A chill ran along her neck as she noticed the cobwebs clustered in each corner. There were no windows and nothing else along the walls. She moved the beam from the light up and down along the four walls. On the third pass her light hit something near the corner.

"Here," she said.

Seth was on the opposite wall and walked over to her. They both knelt down and lit up the floor with their flashlights. There was a cut out in a square approximately two feet by two feet, barely enough to fit a person through. It was a trap door. There was no handle, no lock, no knob, just four quarter-inch slits along the floor that connected into a square.

Seth grabbed the crowbar he brought and wedged the end under one of the slits. Its edge was slightly larger than the opening so it kept slipping. Madison held it in place, and Seth used the other end like a fulcrum and the piece popped loose. He slid the crowbar all the way under until the entire square was loose. Madison picked it up and moved it to the side. It was heavier than she thought it would be. It was not a piece of loose plywood but rather a three inch thick piece of oak. Dust particles rose from it and they waved their hands back and forth to clear the air in front of them. Madison held her nose tight and tried not to sneeze.

Without hesitation, they both shone their lights into the abyss below, but they couldn't see anything but empty space and dust floating to the surface.

"What should we do?" asked Madison.

"I don't see a ladder going down or anything," Seth responded. "We gotta be quick whatever we do. It feels like we've been in here forever."

When the dust started to clear, he noticed the floor of the new room. Except for the random piece of wood on the ground, there wasn't much to see.

"I'm goin down," Seth said. He slid himself over the edge of the drop and looked at Madison. "Drop my flashlight when I get down there."

"I'm coming too," she said.

"No," Seth insisted. "You gotta stay here. I may need your help getting out or what if someone comes. We both can't be down here. I'll be fine."

"Okay," she said, "stay close to the opening where I can see you."

He handed her the flashlight and stuck both legs through the opening. He gave her one last look then pushed off the edge into the blackness below. Madison didn't have to wait very long to hear the thud when his feet hit the bottom. She peeked over the edge and saw that his head was less than a foot from the opening.

"Small room, eh?" she asked.

"Small ceiling, that's for sure." He grabbed the flashlight and winked. "Wish me luck," he said.

He crouched low and disappeared.

The trio from the UK and the twosome from the Secret Service parked their cars about two-hundred yards away from the entrance to Mount Vernon. They had arrived shortly after the gate was opened, but stayed in the shadows until now. Evan was the first out of the backseat of the car and he was quickly followed by Chloe and Max.

"What the hell you think you're doing?" Max asked.

"Getting some air," he responded harshly. He reached into his jacket and pulled out a pack of cigarettes. He offered one to his fellow partners and they both refused. He lit the cigarette and inhaled deeply while looking around. There was a slight breeze that came in off the Potomac that lowered the temperature to around fifty degrees. The trees nearby rustled their leaves causing everyone to feel a great anticipation for what lay ahead.

Evan took a second drag on his cigarette as he watched the feds exit their SUV and walk over.

Kohler spoke first, "What's going on? You guys gotta stay outta sight."

"We know what the hell we're doin!" Max responded. "They can't see us from way up there. Besides, I think it's time we move on them. They've been up there long enough."

"That's a negative," Kohler said, "We stay put until they exit the grounds."

"Shit, man," Evan said, "they could've found something by now and then hid it again. They will come down here, we'll stop them, and they'll tell us they haven't found squat. I say we move."

"I say," Pierce jumped in, "you stay the hell put." Pierce was overweight, that was for sure, but he did his time in the weight room and had been in his share of bar fights before.

"Oh," Evan said, "Mr. Tough Guy has a set of balls now, is that it? You tryin' to impress the lady here?"

"Screw you, the both of you," Chloe said.

"One more word," Pierce insinuated.

"Or what?"

The two men inched closer to each other. Kohler stepped back as did Chloe. Kohler would only jump in if he was double-teamed by Max too. He had seen Pierce in a couple of resisting arrests and knew he had some strength behind that girth. Kohler watched Evan extinguish the cigarette beneath his shoe and look up at Pierce who was still standing two feet away. Evan turned toward the top of the hill and took one step before saying, "I'm headin' up, try and stop me."

Pierce tried.

He closed the distance between them pretty quickly. Evan sensed this would happen and he was slightly uphill, so he was on higher ground and had a small advantage. As the footsteps of Pierce closed in, Evan ducked low and spun, avoiding the overhead punch of Pierce. Evan then thrust his right arm into the soft belly of Pierce who had not seen it coming. He doubled over and his nose ran straight into the uppercut of Evan.

Game. Set. Match.

Kohler made no attempt to help his partner. He was outnumbered two to one, not including the girl. He looked at Pierce on the ground, writhing in pain, holding his nose as blood poured out of both nostrils. He walked over to him, tossed him a handkerchief and said, "I guess we're moving. Let's go Pierce."

Pierce struggled to get up and kept his hand on his nose, pinching the bridge, trying to stop the bleeding. He looked over at Chloe who smirked and he felt embarrassed. He didn't say a word. He wanted to tell

Evan that he was going to kick his ass later. Or that he got lucky. He thought better of it. Why taunt the guy that just kicked *your* own ass?

The five of them moved toward the entrance and the gate which was still open. They turned left and stayed on the walkway. Walking on the grass was too noisy with all of the plants, vegetation and leaves, so using the concrete was more discreet. As they crept up the hill, they could see one flashlight near the entrance to the tomb. Kohler pulled on the jackets of Max and Evan who walked in front of them, indicating to stop.

They stopped and looked back at Kohler who began, "Listen, you two go around the back. Take this trail here," he pointed to his left, "and come up from behind. Pierce and I will approach from the front, right on that flashlight there. You," he pointed to the woman, "stay right here in case anyone escapes and comes running down the hill to the cars. Actually, maybe you should go with one of the men."

"You really don't know me, do ya?" Chloe said. She gazed into his eyes without moving a muscle.

Kohler quickly changed his mind, "Okay, you stay here. Any questions?"

No one had any so he wrapped it up. "Let's move out. First sign of someone running or escaping, shout it out. I want no discharging of weapons. That understood? Last thing I need is the local cops getting a call about gunshots in the park. It'll be all over the news. Okay, let's move."

Two people went left, two went straight, one stayed put.

CHAPTER 23

It was darker than Seth expected. Granted, the room above him was pitch black, but when both flashlights were on, it wasn't terrible. Now, in the pit that was below nine grave markers, his flashlight illuminated a four inch circle of decent light, surrounded by only an additional eight inches of blurred brightness. Still not enough light as he'd like. After dropping into the pit, he surveyed the area looking for four walls. He found three of them. He also shone his flashlight up at the ceiling but found nothing hidden there. The markers on the top were just that, markers.

He moved cautiously around the room, careful to avoid a two by four piece of wood here or a steel rod there. Other than that, the floor was empty. He started with the wall closest to him and felt his way along the edge, shining the flashlight sporadically up and down the wall as he moved to the corner. He heard something behind him and quickly turned his flashlight in the direction of the noise. The sound was like someone smacking their lips, the moisture keeping them together for just a bit longer, but it stopped as the light turned. The flashlight shook in his hand. Maybe it was Madison. Maybe she was walking around up top.

Seth side-stepped toward the corner keeping most of his back against the wall and his flashlight hand stretched in front of him. The room was about fifteen feet long, and it took him almost thirty seconds to cover the full amount. He reached the corner and turned right, again moving with his flashlight scanning ahead of him. There was that sound again. *Smack-smack-smack.* This time he shone the flashlight toward the other side of the room and rapidly moved it around—up and down and left and right but still, he didn't see anything and the sound stopped. Although it was cold, he began to perspire. His hands were clammy and his armpits were damp. He took the sleeve of his jacket and wiped it along his forehead, removing the beads of sweat that had recently formed.

Another thirty seconds and he was at the end of the wall, except this time it didn't have a corner extending right along another wall. This time, the corner made a sharp turn to the left. His flashlight told him there was no wall in front of him and nothing to the left. Seth was now the furthest distance away from the opening where safety was in his grasp. His flashlight fell on nothing as he made his way straight ahead. It wasn't until he walked ten feet that he saw what was making the *Smack-Smack-Smack* sound: rats.

Seth wanted to run. His flashlight found two such creatures sitting on top of a box staring at him. When his flashlight found them, their eyes turned fluorescent red. He felt around in his pocket and brought out the little can of mace he'd bought from the hardware store. He didn't take the flashlight off of the furry little things. He didn't move either. He was paralyzed with fear. Mice, he was okay with, but a rat was like five mice standing on top of each other wearing a rat costume.

One scampered away. He was torn between staying with the rat on the box and following the one that ran away from him. He tailed the rat as it scampered deeper into the underground cavern. He had one hand on the flashlight and the other on the mace. He followed it with his flashlight and took baby steps toward whatever lied ahead. The rat stopped, turned back toward him and stared. It felt like twenty minutes to Seth, but it was only a few seconds before the rat hopped high into the air and landed on something large, about two feet off the ground. Seth took a few more steps and with his flashlight found what the rat had jumped on.

A casket.

Max and Evan darted left into the trees west of the tomb while Kohler and Pierce walked straight ahead, as quietly as they could up the path. After thirty yards, Max could make out the presence of a light up ahead that was moving. It wasn't the spotlights on the ground or the light posts in the air. This was something that was handheld and moving back and forth. He put a finger to his nose and whispered to Evan to move farther left, away from whoever was holding the light. They had to come around back and choke off any escape.

They moved toward the tomb and they were a good fifty yards to its left when they stopped at a small clearing. Max squatted down low and Evan did the same. They spotted the old man and the black security officer from earlier that day standing at the front of the tomb. The old man was shining his flashlight in, trying to see if there was anyone in there. Max noticed that the gates were shut. That meant that whoever was in there, must've gone in another way.

The back?

They looked down the path and saw two figures less than twenty feet from the old guys. Situation in hand, they headed around back.

Kohler and Pierce saw the two Brits out of the corner of their eyes as they crouched low in the woods. When they came into view, they jumped from their cover and ran around the back. They too had been ducking between trees and behind tree stumps. They needed the element of surprise. He didn't know who else was up there, and he certainly didn't want a foot chase to ensue. He held up his hand to Pierce, who was on the other side of the path, indicating to wait. They waited.

They watched the old man shine his flashlight in and they overheard a snippet of conversation.

"They sure are…time."

"Man, its cold."

"We can't…night."

"What…do?"

Neither of them could make out much, but it seemed like they were alone for the moment as the two younger ones went into the tomb. Kohler debated calling the whole thing off. He could run around the back and grab the two Brits before anything happened. Let the kids find it and get them when they came out. What was the difference if they did it now or in fifteen minutes? That all changed when he heard a woman scream.

CHAPTER 24

Madison paced the dark enclosure of the cramped room waiting for some kind of update from Seth. She played with the pink rubber band in her hair at least three times. She kept taking it out, rolling her hair into a ponytail, taking it out, and then letting her hair bounce off her upper-back. She opened the door to go outside once, stepped through, listened for any sounds, and then stepped back in. The first time, she left the door open to let some light into the room. It didn't help much as the night was just as dark as the room. She closed the door, leaving just a crack open, flicked on her flashlight and walked back toward the opening in the floor.

Madison stooped low so that she rested on her heels and whispered Seth's name through the opening, but she received no response. She peeked her head through the opening and was barely able to see the intermittent light coming from his flashlight. That was a good sign at least. Seth was moving. Toward where, she had no idea. It was quiet in the room and she was alone. She even thought about leaving the room and heading to the front to find Willie and Arthur but decided she couldn't leave Seth all alone.

Suddenly, Madison heard the rustling of leaves outside. She got up from her crouch and headed toward the door and listened. The noise was louder now. It was definitely not the wind.

Suddenly, she was afraid.

Then voices. Barely audible, she heard whispers. Willie and Arthur would not be whispering. They would come right to the door calling her name. She made a quick decision and trotted back to the opening in the floor and threw the heavy wooden cover over the opening, blocking all contact with Seth. She had to protect what they found, even if it meant isolating him down there. She killed the flashlight and walked to the corner of the room, farthest from the door.

The voices got louder and she could sense someone was getting closer. She waited in the corner. The door inched open and the first thing she saw was a gun.

She screamed.

The door opened wide and two men stepped in. The gun disappeared in the darkness. One of the men lit a cigarette lighter and she was caught in its' crossfire. It didn't take long for her to recognize the British accents.

"Well, well, well," Max said. "Look what we have here."

Madison said nothing. She put her hand on the can of mace and slowly removed it from her pants pocket.

"What are we doing back here, Miss?" Max asked.

She maintained her silence and watched as the man

with the lighter moved around the small room. He didn't seem to notice the plaques on the floor just yet.

Max became more aggressive. "What," he paused, "are you doing here?"

Madison decided to play it cool. "Nothing," she responded.

"I wouldn't call hiding out in a tomb, nothing, Madison."

Her eyes displayed a look of shock as the man spoke her name.

"Yes, I know you're name, Madison. I know all about you and your little friend, Seth. I know what you're doing here so don't even try to lie to me. My question is this, what did you find?"

She shook her head and said, "Nothing."

"That's probably a lie, right Evan?" he said, looking over at his partner who was still looking around the room. Max looked at her hands, one he could clearly see was holding a flashlight. "Give him your flashlight."

Evan walked over and Madison reluctantly handed it over.

"You probably have found nothing. But, Seth, well, he probably has found something, that's why he's not here. Am I correct?"

Again she said nothing. Her gaze stopped short of the hole in the floor that was now covered. She did not want to reveal his whereabouts.

"Where is he?" Max demanded.

Now she had to lie. "He's outside, looking at the circular courtyard."

Max didn't know whether to believe her or not.

Evan interrupted his thoughts. "Look, I got something."

Max followed the light and found Evan down on one knee looking at the floor. He appeared to be reading something.

"Grave markers," Evan said.

"We didn't find anything," Madison interjected. "Just the markers." She prayed Seth didn't start knocking on the floorboards, signifying his need to get out.

Evan and Max spent a few minutes reading the markers and brushing off the dust of the ones that Madison and Seth had not read. Max looked up at Madison and said, "Do you even know what you're looking for here?"

She shook her head.

"I thought not. I guess you're some kind of treasure hunter, eh? Think you can find the Holy Grail or the next Hope Diamond. Well, my dear, this could be a little more valuable than that."

Evan flashed the light around the room. "There's nothing else here," he said.

"Then let's go find Seth," Max said while standing up. He walked over to Madison and grabbed her arm. "You're coming too."

She thought about the mace in her hand but they had a gun. She took one last glance over her shoulder at the covered hole as they made their way out.

Seth heard the loud thump on the floor above him. He

quickly made his way back to the open room, past the rat and over to where the open hole should have been. It was closed up. He heard small footsteps above and thought about pounding the flashlight on the ceiling. Why cover the hole? There was only one explanation that he could think of. They'd been discovered.

He had to move fast.

He made his way back to the coffin and heard a scream. Madison's scream. Because of the thickness of the wooden floor, she sounded far away, but he knew she was still on the floor above him. He now had a dilemma. Stay there and find something useful, or try and save Madison from whatever it was that was caused her to scream.

He chose the former and proceeded to search the coffin. He moved his light around and saw that this was not the only coffin. There were at least six that he could see, and due to the fact that there were nine markers above him, he guessed he would find the additional three. His focus was only on finding one, Bushrod Washington.

The coffins were all made of wood and well made at that. None of them were crumbling at the corners or falling apart, but they were covered in filth and dust. Cobwebs stretched over them like blankets over a newborn baby. He had to find Bushrod's coffin, as grotesque as that sounded. Would Bushrod really hide something in his own coffin? And who would've put it in there after his death anyway?

Seth felt he was on a wild goose chase, but he had to keep looking. Something was out there and he wanted to find it. The rat had left the first coffin he came upon so he had carte blanche to search its' surroundings. He was not going to open any of them until he had enough reason to do so. He took the sleeve of his jacket and pulled it over his hand and started to clear away some of the spider webs. At the very top of the coffin, on the side, he made out an inscription. The initials ABW were ornately inscribed into the wood. Nothing else. He thought for a second and came to the conclusion that it was Anna Ball Washington, Bushrod's wife.

That was how he got it into his coffin.

According to the small monument in the front, Anna died two days after Bushrod. She certainly could have placed something in his coffin. He scrambled around to the next coffin and saw the initials, AW, Augustine Washington. Seth moved to the one on the other side of Anna, brushing away cobwebs that covered his face as he walked and shining his flashlight ahead of him. He took the sleeve of his jacket and brushed away the spot where he saw the other initials and found him. BW – Bushrod Washington.

"Damn," he said aloud. "It's about time, Bushrod."

He looked at the coffin. It was more rounded in the middle; the others were mostly flat and rectangular. Bushrod's was the same length and type of wood as his wife's. There was an eerie silence, and even the rats were quiet as Seth contemplated his next decision. He decided to check the outside of the coffin first, delaying the inevitable.

You do not desecrate these graves, he heard Willie say in his ear.

Seth walked around the edges of the coffin, using

his left arm to hold the flashlight and his right to brush away the filth and grime so he could see better. Again, he didn't know what he was looking for, but he decided to look anyway. Maybe there was another inscription on the coffin. He made one full turn around the entire coffin, cleaning it as he went. When he came back to the top where the initials were, he had found nothing else. The coffin was sitting on the floor and unless he flipped it over, he was not going to get a good look underneath. If he flipped it over, Mr. Bushrod himself may have come rolling out.

Now what?

It was almost time to open it. Seth was not looking forward to this. The last time he saw an open casket was when his grandmother passed away a few years before. His dad and granddad were silently weeping nearby. He didn't like that experience one bit. Seth didn't know the specifics about decomposition, but he didn't think there would be a body in there. Bones? Maybe. Could bones live forever? Could they survive two hundred years? He was going to find out.

He walked toward the middle of the coffin and turned to face it. The lid looked heavy, most likely heavier than all the others due to the roundness of the top. He grabbed the crowbar out of his backpack and placed his hands on it, one in the front to keep it steady, one in the back to lift the lid. He placed it where he thought it should open and pushed it as far in as it would go under the lip. He used his right hand as a fulcrum and pushed down.

Snap!

Little splinters of wood tumbled about as the

crowbar shattered the lip and it slipped out of his left hand. He tried it again a little further down and got the same result. He had to get the tip of the crowbar further into the coffin. He took it in his right hand and positioned it under the lip a third time. He placed his left hand on the top of the coffin for balance. He pushed with his right hand with all his might and steadied himself with his left.

Snap!

The wood splintered again, only this time it wasn't where the crowbar was, it was where his left hand was, on the top. The top of the rounded coffin was hollow, and Seth's hand went half-way through the splintered wood. He was shocked at first and quickly removed his hand, checking for blood but finding nothing. Seth used the crowbar and started to clear the hole to make it bigger. The wood came apart easily and he was able to shine a flashlight inside. It took only a few seconds to find the leather pouch inside. He removed it and brushed away the dust. It was small and brown and was tied up at the top with twine. As Seth tried to untie it, the rope almost disintegrated in front of his eyes it was so fragile. He opened the top and reached inside.

The brewing process was not a simple one, yet it had existed for thousands of years. The first known beer was documented by the Egyptians in 9500 BC. They used open fermentation and let the natural yeast from the air ferment the sugars in the beer and convert them to alcohol. The Belgian Monks then mastered the process of producing great ale. They used all types of spices that made the beer unique: cinnamon, cardamom, star anise, nutmeg, cloves, orange peel, you name it. President Richard Bowe sat behind his desk in the Oval Office looking at the dark liquid in his glass, seeing perfection from the Monks of Belgium.

It was getting late and he wasn't to be bothered. His wife of only eight years had retired to bed an hour ago. He was lucky to be elected as a newlywed of only a couple years. Most presidents before him had twenty plus years of a stable marriage before even considering the position. At least he didn't sleep around like his Vice-President. Damn Castle. He leaned back in his chair and drained the last of his glass and considered opening a second bottle, until his phone rang.

It was his cell phone. Only a handful of people had the number. His wife of course, the Vice-President, his chief of staff, the secretary of defense and about six others of importance. He had given the number to someone new about three days ago though, the person on the other end of the line.

"Yes," he said.

He listened intently as the caller spoke.

"Okay," he said.

More conversation.

"When was this?" Pause.

"I see," he said.

"Okay, thank you."

More conversation and the President lifted his head to the ceiling. "Yes, I know, you will not be forgotten when this is all over. Your cooperation will be rewarded."

Bowe ended the call and walked around his desk. He opened the door to his office and asked his secret service agent to come inside. The middle-aged man with sharp eyes had a concerned look on his face as his boss brought him inside the Oval Office.

The President looked at him, lowered his voice and said, “Brent, what do you know about Agents Kohler and Pierce?”

CHAPTER 25

The thirty-two foot luxury yacht coming up the Potomac slowly churned through the glass-like surface. A ripple here or a ripple there could not disturb the beauty of a craft like that as it moved in silence through the water. Although it was still spring and the temperatures were cool, this did not stop the owner of this vessel from cruising one of America's finest rivers. Willie had first heard the sound of the engines about thirty seconds before, and they were getting louder.

He turned his head to follow the ship's approach. Willie loved boats. It was his dream as a kid to own a boat and go fishing every weekend. As he looked toward the water, instead of finding a ship, he found two men approaching on foot. He had never seen them before. One of them, the larger one, had a white cloth held to his nose and dry crusty blood covered his cheek. Before he could turn and warn Arthur, the men were on him. There were no guns and no use of force either.

The men approached and as Arthur turned to see what was coming, they put their fingers to their lips, signaling silence.

"We'll start," Kohler said. "First, don't start screaming because there's nobody here. Do that, and I'll be the first to call the cops because you're trespassing on federal property. Second, where the hell are your partners? The girl and your grandson?"

Willie looked back at Arthur and said, "You know these guys?"

"Dah," Arthur snarled, "they don't know anything. They're just harassing us."

"Then what are you doing here in the middle of the night, old man?"

Willie decided to speak, "I'm giving him an after-hours tour."

Kohler chuckled. "Okay, let's call it in, if that's what it is. Pierce," he snapped his fingers, "do the honors."

Pierce picked up his phone and pretended to dial.

"Okay, wait," Arthur pleaded. He put his head down as he spoke, "We haven't found anything if that's what you're wondering. And, I hope that scream a few minutes ago wasn't that girl with your cronies."

"I told ya we should've went back there to check on her," Willie said.

"Why don't we all go back there?" Kohler said, opening up his jacket to reveal the pistol holstered to his chest.

The two older men lowered their heads and were pushed from behind by Pierce, around the side toward the back of the tomb.

Madison calmly called Seth's name in the darkness. She led them back to the circular grove where they saw the marker for the Afro-American slaves that were reportedly buried here. Evan still had the flashlight and was on the outskirts of the circle, scanning his light both inside and outside.

"You're screwin with us," Evan said, clearly frustrated.

Madison had to play it cool for a little while longer and hope that Seth found something and escaped. She could play this game all night with this little prick. "I don't know where he is, we split up."

Max stood in the center of the grassy arena looking around as Madison and Evan argued. Something wasn't right. They had found no one, and he knew no man would leave a hot chick like Madison by herself in the dark. He was about to say something when he heard footsteps approaching from behind. He swung his gun in the direction of the tomb.

The two old men approached, followed by the feds.

"Welcome to the party," Max said. "Glad you two could join us."

Evan walked towards the center and said, specifically to Pierce, "Wow, I can't believe you could handle these two geezers. How's your nose?"

Pierce didn't even look at him.

Max held up his hands and said to all of them, "Alright, where is he?"

Everyone looked around at each other and no one

spoke a word. Arthur looked at Madison who gave a slight nod of her head in the direction of the tomb.

"Well guess what?" Max said. "No one goes anywhere until he comes back here."

November 25, 1829

Bushrod knew his days were numbered. He was in Philadelphia at the time and could not even make it back to his estate in Mount Vernon. His wife, Anna, was at his side weeping. He'd been sick before but not like this. At age sixty-seven, something just didn't feel right and he had accepted the fact that his time had come.

"Anna," he said softly. "I want you to do something for me."

His wife looked over at him and touched his cheek with her hand. "Anything dear, what is it?"

"I need you to draft a letter for me," he said.

She grabbed the quill and a piece of paper from the desk and waited for him to speak.

"If you are reading this, you have followed my trail very well. Unfortunately for you, I left what you are looking for in the hands of a new generation. This will ensure the safety of the document that my uncle kept hidden all these years. The safest place for such a document lies with my Uncle George's only child by blood."

"What is this you speak of?" asked Anna.

"You need not worry about such matters, my dear. Please put that in the safety pouch your mother left you and have the caretaker put it away where I instructed him."

Anna was confused but did as he told her. She watched as her husband lay still and closed his eyes.

CHAPTER 26

Seth read the note a second time, looking for something else. *"If you are reading this, you have followed my trail very well. Unfortunately for you, I left what you are looking for in the hands of a new generation. This will ensure the safety of the document that my uncle kept hidden all these years. The safest place for such a document lies with my Uncle George's only child by blood."* He had come all this way and still hadn't found anything. What if the next note led him to another note and so on and so on? What if there was no document? He could not get discouraged. He had to be positive when he told the others what he had found. He folded the note, put it back in the leather pouch and stuffed it in his jacket. He moved back out of the dark cavern and into the empty room.

Since the small opening in the ceiling was closed, it took him a few moments to find it. He raised his arms and pushed it open and to the side of the floor above him. Seth jumped up and grabbed a hold of the floor and called out Madison's name but he received no reply. The room was dark and she was gone. He pulled himself out of the hole and replaced the cover. He decided to take the pouch out of his jacket and remove the note. He took off one of his shoes, placed the note in, and then replaced his shoe on his foot. He left the pouch in the corner of the room and opened the door ever so slightly.

Seth heard voices coming from outside but they seemed to be in the distance. He heard men asking where he was and Madison replying that he was here just a moment ago. He took a look outside and saw through the trees that they were standing near the slave memorial. He opened the door all the way, stepped outside and closed the door. He crept through the woods and circled around the back of the group. When he got close he said, "I'm right here."

All of them gazed at him with wonderment.

"Well, well," Max said. "What'd ya find, mate?"

Seth held out his hands and said, "Nothin."

"Come on," Evan chimed in, "you've been gone this whole time and found nothing?"

"Search him," Max said to Evan.

Evan walked over to Seth and started patting him down. He reached into his jacket pockets, felt his jeans pockets and found nothing.

"He's clean," Evan said.

"Ah, Christ," Max said, "Now what?"

All of a sudden, Max heard his name being called from a distance. He turned in the direction of the tomb and listened. "MAX!" a woman called. He recognized it was Chloe.

"Over here, round back!" he yelled.

Chloe appeared through the trees jogging, her red hair bouncing off her shoulders. She stopped and caught her breath before saying, "Cop car just pulled in."

"Shit," Kohler said. "Let's go Pierce." He grabbed him by the jacket and pushed him toward the exit and they ran off.

"Good luck explaining yourself," Max said to Seth. The three Brits ran off in the same direction as the Feds.

"I'll handle this," Willie said. He walked toward the exit and they followed him out.

"Well?" Madison asked Seth.

"I didn't find whatever Washington hid," he said.

"Damn, all this for nothing," she responded.

"I did find something though. We're closer," he said.

"What? What did you find?" she asked.

They walked quickly down the path. Willie stopped and told them to keep going and then joined in behind them.

"I'll tell you in a minute," Seth said.

They got to the bottom of the hill and saw a police officer looking in Madison's car with a flashlight. He saw them approach and put his hand on his gun.

"It's all right officer," Willie said, opening up his jacket to reveal his uniform. "Mount Vernon security. I got everything under control."

"What's going on?" the officer asked.

"They were just looking at the tomb. They claim they drove all day from Pennsylvania, Pittsburgh I think they said. When they arrived, the gates were closed. I was doing my nightly drive-by back to my house and saw the car parked here. They said they were related to someone buried up there and wanted to see the grave. No harm no foul."

The officer was suspicious but didn't see any real threat. He bid them good night and told them to come back in the morning when the park was open. They waved at him as he drove off.

"Thanks Willie," Arthur said.

"What'd you find?" Willie asked Seth.

Seth took off his shoe and lifted out the folded note and handed it to Willie. He opened the note and put a hand to his chest.

"Jesus H Christ," he said.

Madison grabbed the note and with Arthur reading over her shoulder she read it out loud. "If you are reading this, you have followed my trail very well. Unfortunately for you, I left what you are looking for in the hands of a new generation. This will ensure the safety of the document that my uncle kept hidden all these years. The safest place for such a document lies with my Uncle George's only child by blood."

"That's it, another dead end," Arthur said.

"It's no dead end," Willie replied.

"What?" he asked.

"Remember when I told you I was related to George Washington?"

The President had to keep his nose clean in some

respect. After his closest agent Brent had told him about Kohler and Pierce, he knew he needed to make a move. He remembered Kohler, that was for sure. What Kohler had on him could ruin him. The President wanted to now return the favor and bring about a little fair play.

After the call he received, he had Brent contact the Mount Vernon Police Department with an anonymous tip about some vandals on the property. The person who tipped him off was owed a favor, what he could only guess. He was sure it could be handled by someone on his staff. A position in the White House or an aide to an important political figure was done all the time. Favors were a part of the political process.

Brent called him shortly thereafter informing him that the police checked on the estate and found that there was a security guard on hand and a couple of tourists, nothing to write home about. Something or someone had gotten away, he thought. The vice-president was up to something. If he was snooping around, there was no telling what he would turn up, but the president had more ears and eyes in places than the VP had and more allies too. Plus, the caller from earlier was on his side.

"Ever hear of West Ford?" Willie asked.

They were back in separate cars on their way to Willie's house. It was after eleven but with this latest revelation, no one was tired, not even Arthur. Willie poured two more drinks for himself and Arthur, and

Seth and Madison asked for water. They moved back into the living room and sat as they had hours before.

No one responded to the question Willie asked.

“West Ford was born on the Bushfield Plantation back in 1784. He was a slave, as most if not all Afro-Americans were in that time period. More importantly, he was a slave on the plantation owned by John Washington, George’s brother. George frequented his brother’s estate and West Ford served as his personal attendant. George took a liking to the boy and often brought him out riding and hunting.”

“George owned slaves?” Madison asked, much to her chagrin.

“Most certainly, my dear. All white landowners owned slaves back then. George was not a big proponent and in fact asked in his will that slaves be freed. West Ford came to live at Mount Vernon and was actually granted his freedom in 1806. He married his wife and raised their four children at Mount Vernon. He was so well liked that Bushrod willed him one hundred sixty acres of land near Mount Vernon.”

“Wow, pretty good for a slave,” Arthur said.

“Damn good at that,” Willie replied. “He eventually sold that land and bought over two hundred acres nearby. He divided the acres between his four children and they each lived there. When he died at the ripe old age of seventy-nine, there were articles written about the man with such distinction. This was in 1863. He was buried in the tomb we were just at.”

“Get outta here!” Arthur exclaimed, and then downed his drink.

Willie took a sip of his own drink. “Yes, it is true.

Most of the slaves were buried in the circular grove we were at today, but West received the royal treatment along with others from the Washington family."

"Why was a black man in that day given such preferential treatment?" Madison asked.

Willie smiled at them all and leaned forward on his elbows, cradling the glass between both hands. "Because West Ford was George Washington's son."

Tick – Tick – Tick

That was the only sound in the room coming from the clock on the mantle. After ten ticks, the two hands reached up together and the clock struck midnight, jarring them all from the news that was just bestowed upon them.

"You shittin us Dub-Dub?" Arthur asked.

He chuckled. "No, I'm not. Now, no one wants you to believe it, and everyone has tried to deny it and cover it up. Some historians claim it was his brother John's son, but family members disagree. A slave woman named Venus confided in John's wife Hanna and told her that she was sleeping with George when he came to their plantation."

"I need another drink," Arthur said. He went into the kitchen grabbing Willie's glass on the way and poured them another splash of the wicked concoction that his friend made.

"I thought it was reported that Washington was sterile?"

"Well, that's an unproven rumor," Willie said. "Maybe they wanted to cover the fact that Washington had a child out of wedlock. A black child at that."

"Then what? How did this not all come out?" Seth

asked.

"Oh, it has come out. The story broke in 1998 and it was covered in news reports, magazines and newspapers, then it just fizzled away. There was a book about it a few years ago by some relatives, but it wasn't talked about that much."

"Why not?" Seth asked.

"Because people in high places don't want you to learn the fact that the father of this country was sleeping with a black slave and had an illegitimate child. That's why. And who would believe it?"

"So Ford's children, what happened to them?" Madison asked.

"They had two boys and two girls. I think they were military men back then. Then their children had children and so on and so forth."

"Wait," Arthur asked, "how do you know all this? Wait, no…"

Willie leaned back in his chair and smiled at Arthur.

"Oh!" Madison said, "No way!"

"What?" Seth asked.

"It's true," Willie said. "I am related to West Ford, he was my great-great-great-great-grandfather."

CHAPTER 27

The Deputy Prime Minister of England was up at five am just like every other day. He jumped out of his lonely bed and stretched his arms high over his head. He flipped on the television to see what the London Exchange was primed to do that day. The Japanese market was having a solid day which meant London should parallel their success. He threw on black gym shorts and a gray t-shirt that hugged his tight torso and collapsed onto the floor of his bedroom. He didn't open the shade of his bedroom but instead relied on the glow of the television.

Keeping in shape was a priority for him, and he busted out fifty crunches followed by fifty push-ups. He got up and went over to his closet door and opened it. On the top of the door was a pull-up bar. He grabbed it and knocked out thirteen pull-ups until he felt the burn. In the corner of his massive bedroom was a treadmill. After putting on socks and running shoes, he fired up the treadmill to level 8.0 and was flying through five miles in less than thirty-five minutes.

After he showered and dressed in a tailored Armani suit, he poured himself a to-go cup of coffee, grabbed his laptop bag and headed out the door. His driver was already parked out front of the building, as he was every day at precisely 6:30 am. The man opened the door for him and Greg Bannister entered the car.

At age forty-two, Bannister looked thirty-two. Not only was he in impeccable shape, he had a full head of light brown hair, did not need glasses or contacts to cover his brown eyes, went tanning once a week to maintain a slight hint of color, had a manicure once a month, and also whitened his teeth twice a year. All of this contributed to the fact that he was voted as the second most eligible bachelor in Britain, behind the Prince of course. Bannister didn't care. He made enough money and got laid whenever he wanted.

The Deputy Prime Minister position made him second-in-command of Great Britain, behind the Prime Minister, Alec Wood. Wood was in his late fifties and was popular with the Liberal Democrats in the country. Bannister played the role of supporting Wood, but as soon as he had his way, Wood would be out of office, sooner rather than later. The thing about being the Deputy PM was that your role if something ever happened to the PM was not guaranteed. In America if The President of the United States died or was impeached, the VP automatically took over. In Great Britain, if the PM could not perform his duties, the cabinet would decide his replacement. Even the Queen of England had been known to express her support in favor of one candidate or another.

Bannister had his laptop open in the back of the car and picked up his personal cell phone. He dialed Max Church's number and waited a few seconds for the connection to go through.

"Max here," he heard on the other end.

"What's going on?" Bannister said.

"Right now we're sitting on our duffs in a cold car outside a house."

"Whose house?"

"Some security guy from Mount Vernon. The kid, the girl and the old man are inside. We followed them here after the cops were snooping around Mount Vernon. We had to get outta there."

"Did they find it?" Bannister asked.

"Don't think so," Max responded. "The kid was gone for a little bit but we searched him and didn't turn up anything."

"Stay on them."

"We are, don't worry."

"It's my job to worry, Max."

He ended the call and looked out the window as the sun was rising above the hills to the east. The weather man on the TV this morning said it was going to be sixty and sunny in London. A perfect day.

"So you never heard of this so-called document before?" Seth asked Willie.

They were still seated in the living room. Madison had moved to the floor with her head propped up on two pillows. Arthur was drifting off, and Willie was tired of all the questions. It was late and everyone was exhausted.

"I've heard of it Seth, that's why I was looking for it until someone swiped it from me," he said, glancing over at Arthur who stirred.

"But no one in your family ever talked about it?"

"Never," he said. "I'd have known too. We talked about that journal all the time. If someone in my family had the document in question, I'd have it right next to me."

Seth put his face in his hands and leaned over so that he was looking at the ground. He was emotionally invested in this now. There was no walking away. He looked to his left and saw that Madison was out cold. Across from him, his granddad was snoring away.

"I have a spare bedroom upstairs for you and Madison, if you like," Willie said. "I'll pull out the couch for the old man here."

"Let's just review this real quick," Seth said.

Willie sighed but said okay.

"George Washington did something or knew something that he was not proud of that he kept to himself. Remember the journal, it said, 'It is with great displeasure that I am writing this. Let me tell you that I did what I did under great duress and for the betterment of the country and my family'."

Willie nodded, "Then he hid the document or whatever it was in the Betsy Ross house, correct?"

"Yep, and he gave the journal to Bushrod who deciphered the journal and went to the Ross house and moved the document to Valley Forge. But, he changed his mind and he thought this document was so important, he wanted to bury it with him. Then, he found out that his Uncle George had a child named West Ford. He thought this secret must stay in the family so he left it with West Ford."

"That's about the gist of it. Time for bed," Willie said, getting up from the chair. He nudged Arthur who got up and went to the bathroom.

"Damn," Seth said. "What did West Ford do with it?"

"That," Willie said as the night came to an end, "is the million dollar question."

Sleep came quickly for Seth although his mind was racing. He'd woken Madison and they went upstairs and crashed in the guest bedroom. It had been a long day, and this was Madison's second night in a row away from her own bed, Seth's third since he spent the night on Madison's couch. The bright morning sun did not even wake them and everyone slept until after eight o'clock. He left Madison half-sleeping, half-awake and went downstairs. When he stepped into the kitchen he was greeted by Willie who was making coffee and discovered his granddad still sleeping on the pull-out couch in the living room.

"I've been thinking Willie," Seth began.

"Don't hurt yourself kid," Willie replied.

"Since no one in your family ever mentioned this document, is it possible that West Ford gave it to someone else? Or, better yet, buried it with him?"

Willie was pulling coffee mugs and sugar from the white cabinets and milk from the refrigerator. "Anything's possible, boy. I just don't think it's with the family anymore. And, if it was so important, why bury it? Why not give it to someone of importance? Remember, Washington died in 1799 and West Ford died sixty four years later. A lot can change in that time. What I think, is that this document or whatever it is, did not go to the grave with West Ford. It was too important."

Seth nodded. Willie poured two cups of coffee and pushed one across the counter to Seth who added sugar and milk.

"So," Seth began, "let's assume West Ford received this document from Bushrod who said, 'this is very important and I want you to have it'. Ford reads the document and hides it away. Then, he's on his deathbed, right, just like George was and realizes, 'Hey, I gotta pass this thing along.'"

"Yep, now who does he give it to then?" Madison asked, coming through the hallway into the kitchen.

"Morning, miss, can I get you a cup?" Willie asked.

"Sure, thanks," she replied.

"So who does he give it to Madison?" Seth asked.

She took the cup from Willie and added a drop of milk. "Well, I think it would have to be someone who was near him on his deathbed, right? Wife, kids, brother?"

"We're discounting the family. The document is too important, and Willie said none of his family members have ever seen it," Seth said.

"Huh," Madison said, "well, then it could be anyone. Willie, you said West died at Mount Vernon right?"

"Yes ma'am, July 20th, 1863," Willie replied.

"There you have it," Madison said. "We need to find every person that was at Mount Vernon to visit West Ford the last two months of his life."

"Piece of cake!" Arthur said, rising from the living room and clasping his hands together.

It was a long night for Max, Evan and Chloe but an even longer one for Kohler and Pierce. Max had thrown in the towel at around one in the morning and left the surveillance to find a hotel. He planted his own surveillance on Kohler's SUV and they monitored the action from the comfort of their hotel room. Kohler and Pierce pulled out right after them and went home to the comfort of their own beds in their own houses. They slipped another tracking device on the old man's truck and monitored both cars.

Next up, Kohler was going to put a trace on all of their calls.

CHAPTER 28

The Mount Vernon Ladies Association was formed in 1858 to preserve the historical site where George Washington lived and ultimately passed away. They made the land available for the public to come and visit and the society still exists today, 150 years later. They had collected letters between George and Martha, photographs and artists' renditions of the Washingtons. Most importantly, Willie knew, they kept the guest registry of all the important guests who had ever visited the estate.

When the offices opened at nine o'clock, Willie placed a call to his friend in the society, Betty Timmons.

"Betty," Willie began, "hey, it's Willie. How are you?"

"Good, Willie, good. What can I do for you?"

"Well Betty, my grandson is doing a report on Mount Vernon, specifically the time period that you fine folks took over Mount Vernon. I was wondering if you had the guest registry for 1863."

"Huh," she said. "That is a little unusual, but I'm sure we have it here on both microfiche and in soft copy."

"Soft copy?" Willie asked.

"Yes, on a computer."

"Oh, I see, great."

"What is it you want this for again?" she asked.

"They are public records, are they not?"

"Why yes, they are. I was just wondering why you needed them."

Willie gave her no more information than what was necessary. "Can you send me the registry from 1863?"

She hesitated. "Well, I guess there's no harm in that. Where should I send them?"

"To my email." Willie gave her his email address and hung up the phone.

"You have email?" Arthur asked.

"Yeah, gotta have email these days, especially if I want to talk to my daughter."

Willie made them all scrambled eggs, Canadian bacon and toast. All of the men chowed down, but Madison passed on the bacon.

Willie paced back and forth into the office checking his computer every ten minutes for the email from Betty. At around ten o'clock, he received it.

"Here we go," he said, pulling up the document. It was an Excel spreadsheet with multiple columns showing the person's name, guests they brought, date and time of entry and date and time of departure. "Lotta names here," he said.

He printed all sixteen pages out and narrowed the list to the dates from May of 1863 to the day West Ford died on July 20th. Willie divided the remaining eight pages and gave them each two sheets of paper. Arthur sat in a chair and Madison and Seth sat on the floor, scanning over the documents.

"We don't even know who we're looking for," Madison said.

"You'll know it when you see it," Seth added. "We're looking for someone important. A Washington, a Ford, someone associated with this crazy chase."

Minutes passed and frustration set in for Arthur. "I've got nothing here," he said.

"Same here," Madison said.

"I'm just about done too," Seth said.

Willie scrutinized his list. He finished page one, and all eyes were on him as he flipped to the next page. His dark eyes darted left and right reading each entry with a thoughtful gaze. His eyes stopped about halfway down the page. His eyes not only stopped they expanded to almost twice their size, the whites increasing enough to show the red veins on either side.

"What?" Arthur asked.

"I think," Willie said.

"What?" Seth begged.

"On July 18th, just two days before West Ford passed away he was visited by one important fellow."

"Who?" Madison asked.

Willie put the sheets down on the table and folded his hands over his chest. "Just the sixteenth President of the United States, Mr. Abraham Lincoln."

July 18, 1863

Two large powerful dark brown horses pulled the second carriage around the bend to the front of Mount Vernon. The first carriage had stopped at the rear of the house and another carriage came around to the front of the large house. At fifty-four years of age, President Lincoln was still limber enough to take the large step out of the carriage and onto the gravel drive without any assistance. He turned, extended his hand, and helped his wife Mary out of the coach. They made their way up the few steps of the house and turned to take in the beautiful view of the Potomac. Three men from the other carriage, the President's security detail, followed closely behind.

The door opened and they were greeted by two servants dressed in white. They paid their respects to the President and led them through the hallway and up the steps to the first bedroom on the right. The President walked in and touched the man on the bed.

"Mr. President," the man said in a hard gravelly voice. He had lost a lot of weight these past few months. Large tufts of white hair haphazardly crisscrossed his skull. He looked up at Abraham Lincoln who stood at his side.

"Mr. Ford, it is a pleasure to speak with you.

You are an inspiration to us all, black and white."

"No, Mr. President, you're the inspiration. You have freed thousands of us, and thousands more when this war is over. God will bestow upon you many great blessings."

They talked for a few more minutes on the effect of the Emancipation Proclamation that was signed a few months earlier, essentially ending slavery. Mary did not say much and just listened.

During a brief break in conversation, West Ford asked Lincoln if he could speak to him alone. He nodded to his wife Mary and she left the room.

"Mr. President, I have the document," Ford said.

"What document?" Lincoln asked.

"*The* document sir. The one George Washington himself signed. I've had it since Mr. Bushrod passed away sir. Why it was given to me, I'm sure you've known by now."

"Well, I must say thank you for keeping it so long, and more importantly, keeping its contents secret."

"That was an honor. Mr. Washington was a great man, and I understand why he did not reveal his identity as a father to me. May I ask a question, Mr. President?" the ailing man continued without waiting for a reply. "If I had the document all this time, how did you know about it?"

Lincoln leaned forward in the chair and replied, "Every President before me has passed on its contents to one another. Both the Vice-President and I know its secret, just in case anything happened to one of us. Now, if something happened to both of us, well, the folks on the other side of the Atlantic would raise a stink."

"So it's true?" Ford asked.

"Sure is," Lincoln replied. "Even seventy years later and probably seventy years from now."

Ford told him where in the house to find the document and Lincoln brought it with him back to the White House. West Ford died two days later.

"What?" Seth exclaimed. They all looked at Willie who held the printed out roster in his hand and read from it again.

"Says here, on July 18th at 12:30 pm, Abraham Lincoln was signed into Mount Vernon. Also at 12:30 were four other names. One of them his wife Mary, the other three I don't seem to recognize."

"Wow," Madison said.

"Yeah, President Abraham Lincoln," Arthur said.

"So," Seth said, the wheels turning in his head, "are we to assume that West Ford gave Lincoln the document?"

"Well," Madison said, "we have nothing else to go by so that's the route I'm taking."

"So assuming Ford gave him the document, what did Lincoln do with it?" Seth asked.

"The hell if I know," Willie said, leaning back in

the chair.

"Let's put our heads together people," Seth insisted. "In 1863, The President had a document in his hand that was drafted by George Washington. At least, we think he did. Lincoln put it somewhere. Did he have any children?" he asked no one in particular.

A lot of shrugs around the room. No one knew.

"We'll look that up in a minute. What else? Had he given it to his wife, Mary? And if he did, what did she do with it? Geez, we're never going to get anywhere."

"Arthur, Willie, you guys know anything about Lincoln?" Madison asked.

Arthur was the first to speak up. "Whoa, whoa. I know we're getting on in years but we weren't alive in the 1860's dear."

"You know what I meant," she said.

Now it was Willie's turn. "He was a great President and an even better man."

"How so?" Madison asked.

"Look at it from a black man's point of view. He freed the slaves. This issue was the main reason for the Civil War and he didn't care. Washington wanted the slaves freed, he said so in his will, and they still were not free until sixty years after his death. Course, we still had issues until the Civil Rights movement one hundred years later." Willie shook his head. "Lincoln died too early."

"John Wilkes Booth," Arthur said.

Madison fired up her laptop while finishing her coffee. Seth moved in close to her and watched as she waited for the wireless internet connection Willie had installed for his daughter.

"All right," Seth said, "so we know he freed the slaves, what else?"

"The Gettysburg Address," Arthur said.

"Right, good." He had Madison pull up a Word document and she started typing in everything that was thrown out there.

"Emancipation Proclamation," Willie said.

"Good, keep 'em comin'," Seth said.

Madison searched Wikipedia for Lincoln and read out the first fact she found. "Says here he created the Secret Service."

"Write it down, when was that?"

"April 14, 1865," she replied.

"Huh," Willie said, "that's a little ominous."

"Why?" Seth asked.

"He was shot that same day and died the next day."

"That is weird. Maybe he should have formed the Secret Service the week before."

"Ford," Arthur said suddenly.

"What about West Ford?" Seth asked.

"No, not him. Ford's *Theater*," he said. "The place of his assassination."

Madison stopped typing and all eyes focused on the old man who tapped his skull and smiled. "I still got a little left up here you know."

"That's good, Arthur," Willie said.

"Yes," Seth said. "Lincoln had a ton of respect for West Ford. He paid him a visit on his death bed for cryin' out loud. Madison, find out if Lincoln went to Ford's Theater before he was assassinated."

She typed away and scrolled through various

websites. "For one thing, Ford's Theater was not named after West Ford."

"That's fine," Seth said. "It's still the name Ford that provides the link we need."

"Says here that Lincoln first went to the theater in 1862 and frequented it often until his death in 1865," Madison read aloud from her computer.

"That means he definitely could've hidden the document some time before he died."

"That theater has been renovated probably a couple of times," Willie said. "There could be nothing left of what was there in 1863."

"Only one way to find out," Seth insisted.

CHAPTER 29

Both cars were now positioned about a block apart from Willie's suburban home. It was an overcast day, and the cool temperature caused the drivers to turn on the ignition and fire up the heat every fifteen minutes or so. Kohler had gotten a trace on two calls from the home this morning. The first an outgoing call to Mount Vernon, the second, a call back from the same number. Neither call told him much. Could be just the old man calling out of work or phoning a friend. They decided to sit and wait.

Vice President Castle called Kohler's phone and he updated the man.

"I'm getting impatient," the VP said.

"You are? Try sitting in a freezing car waiting to follow someone to God knows where." Kohler wanted to say more but caught himself. This was the Vice President after all. "Sorry sir," he said. "We're just tired."

"I understand. Hopefully these folks are pretty close to finding it."

"Sir, can I ask a question?" Kohler stated.

"If it's not about what's in the document."

Kohler sighed, "Then I guess I don't have a question."

"Listen Kohler, you will know about this soon enough. It will be broadcast throughout the world. I'll give you a little teaser though."

"Yeah," Kohler perked up.

"There are actually two of these documents, and someone found one in London a few months ago. I was contacted and told about a second document. They're identical in nature. But, they will not reveal the document until we find the same one over here."

"How did you get on the fact that these people we're following were looking for the document?"

"Good question. I did my homework. Found out a little about the journal. I had Bunkley follow that Willie Wright guy and search his house but he turned up nothing. Started following the daughter around, nothing. Bunkley's the computer geek so he looked into Willie's past and saw he was in the Marines. Did a thorough search of his platoon and came up with Arthur Layton. Didn't think nothing of it but we still had to investigate it. Turns out, he stole some liquor at the old folks home he's in, got wasted and told a nurse that he once had a book written by Washington. The nurse told Bunkley and you guys came into the picture."

"Interesting," Kohler said.

"Yeah, so find it already, would you? You guys will be at the top of my list when this all comes out."

<><><><><>

The drive over to 511 10th Street Northwest in DC traffic took a long time. It usually didn't matter the time of day with how bad traffic was, Willie explained in the car. They left Madison's car at his house and they piled into the pickup truck with the extended cab. He told them to never live in DC, he didn't want another car on the road. The beltway was always jammed day and night. It seemed like people got out of work at three in the afternoon he complained.

There was no good time to enter the heart of DC. If it was during the week, the roads were mobbed with commuters, buses, and messengers on bikes. On the weekend, tourists from all over the world came to see the White House, the Capitol and countless museums in the area. Ford's Theater was certainly an attraction, but it didn't garner as much attention as the Smithsonian or other national landmarks. They pulled down 10th Street Northwest and Willie parked his pickup in a parking garage and they walked the short distance to the front of Ford's Theater.

It was a three-story red brick building with a domed roof that possibly doubled as an attic or storage area. The outside of the first floor was white concrete with five circular archways that led to five sets of double doors. The glass entryway before the theater on the left was where tourists first walked in. They entered the building and were given four tickets to the museum and the theater, free of charge.

"Please turn your cell phones off or to vibrate," the

aging security guard said. "Cameras are allowed but not during the presentation which starts in about twenty minutes. The presentation is optional and is located in the main theater. Have a splendid day."

He raised the retractable cord and allowed them to proceed down a ramp toward the museum. They went down a short flight of stairs and started their tour. A few other people were milling about and Seth took notice of everyone here. A young couple and what looked like grandparents and their two grandchildren were the only ones so far that he noticed.

It was dark and quiet in the museum, except for the televisions playing historical features throughout their walk. They proceeded onward through the maze that described Abraham Lincoln's life from childhood through his Presidency. His dealings with former slave Frederick Douglas, the Gettysburg Address, and the Emancipation Proclamation were all showcased throughout the floor with plaques and pictures on the walls. Actual artifacts from everything to do with Lincoln including White House plates were behind glass cases.

They finally turned the corner and started to read about John Wilkes Booth and the plot to kill Lincoln.

"Actually," Willie said, "he first tried to kidnap him. Look here." He pointed to the wall and they read that Booth did indeed plot to kidnap the President, but after General Lee surrendered at Appomattox Court House, the point was moot. So, he decided to kill the President.

"Look, they were also going to kill others too," Madison read aloud, "They were going to murder Vice-

President Andrew Johnson and Secretary of State William Seward. Wow."

Willie again chimed in, "Seward ended up being stabbed but survived, and the guy that was supposed to kill Johnson got scared and failed to carry out his portion of the plot."

"It seems like such a long time ago," Seth said, "but really, it was only one hundred and fifty years ago."

They turned around to the back of the display and there positioned in the center of the wall was the gun that killed President Abraham Lincoln.

"It's so tiny," Madison said.

Indeed it was. The brown handle of the gun was small and extended only two inches under the trigger and the steel barrel was only about three inches in length.

"Says that Booth dropped the gun after shooting Lincoln," Seth said, reading the inscription outside the glass enclosure.

Below the gun outside of the glass case was a round lead ball and they read that this was the size of the bullet that killed the President. This was also small, weighing only about an ounce. They proceeded along the corridor and next came a timeline of April 14, 1865. On one side of the wall was Lincoln's timeline from eight in the morning until ten that night. On the other side was Booth's timeline. An eerie silence fell into the room as the four of them read to themselves.

They took the elevator up to the second floor and walked along the back row of seats in the theater toward Lincoln's box. They looked below at the theater and saw a crowd of about fifteen people scattered among the seats listening to a gray-haired woman speaking on stage.

"Lincoln was actually late to the theater and the play, *Our American Cousin*, had already started. But when the President arrived, the play stopped and everyone applauded as the orchestra played *Hail to the Chief*."

Seth led them down along the row of seats and waited their turn to enter the narrow passageway that led to the President's private box.

"John Parker," the woman on stage continued, "a Washington police officer, waited outside the balcony box while the President and his guests, his wife Mary of course, Clara Harris, and Major Henry Rathbone watched the play inside. Ironically enough, Lincoln created the Secret Service that very day, but no one had been put into place just yet outside of his normal security staff.

"During intermission, Parker decided to leave the theater and get a drink with Lincoln's footman and coachman and did not return. At approximately ten-fifteen that night, John Wilkes Booth entered Lincoln's private box and secured a piece of wood against the door so it could not be opened from the outside. He pulled out a small Deringer and waited until the precise moment of laughter from the crowd and shot Lincoln in the back of the head. He then dropped the gun and stabbed Major Rathbone before he could react. It was said that Booth shouted 'Sic Semper Tyrannis!' meaning Thus Always to Tyrants. He then jumped from that balcony onto this stage, breaking his leg in the process, and escaped into the night."

"Fascinating," Willie said. It was their turn and they made their way toward the viewing box. There were two doors and both were locked. The first door on their left was shielded in hard plastic from the waist up to allow visitors to view the famous box. The plastic was even curved outward so that you could stick your head in and see more clearly.

The box was very small. It had two high-backed chairs and a small bench, both covered in dark red velvet. The view to the stage was such that when seated in the box, the President could almost look straight down on the actors. Willie and Arthur stepped away as Madison and Seth took their turn looking into the room.

"How did Booth get into the theater?" someone asked from the crowd.

"Good question," the woman replied. "Booth was actually an actor right here at this very theater. He tied up his horse around back and was let inside. He came here all the time so he did not arouse any suspicion."

Seth and Madison joined the other men and they walked back to the top of the spiral staircase and went to the lower level to listen to the remainder of the talk that was just wrapping up.

"In fact," the woman said, "there's going to be an auction right here for about fifteen items from this Theater that were left over from the renovation."

"When is this?" Seth asked.

"Tonight at seven pm," she replied. "If you check at the front, they can probably let you know if there are any tickets left."

"Thanks," Seth said. "Do you know if there are

going to be any items for sale that were related to President Lincoln?"

"Let's see, there are a few items left, but I don't know if any are going to be auctioned off. Let me check." She reached under her lectern and returned with a binder. After flipping through a couple of pages she stopped and drew her finger down a list. "Hmm, it looks like they are auctioning off two things. The red velvet rope and the actual door to his box."

"Thank you," Seth said. They walked off toward the ticket booth in the front. "Do you think the door could be it?"

Madison walked alongside and shrugged her shoulder. "I have no idea. It could be anywhere. It was his private box and no one else entered it. What better place?"

They reached the ticket booth and found that indeed there were tickets left so they bought four tickets to the auction. They were instructed to be in the theater at six-thirty sharp and to have a checkbook, ID, and two major credit cards if they wished to purchase anything.

"How are we going to come up with the money to buy the door?" Seth asked.

"I'll take care of that, son," his granddad replied.

Seth started to ask a question, but his granddad held up his hand in protest and that was the end of the discussion. It was just past twelve o'clock so they went over to the Hard Rock Café on the corner and ordered iced tea and sandwiches. Soon they were back outside with a few hours to kill before the auction.

"It'll take too long to drive back to my house then all the way over here in this traffic," Willie said.

"What's nearby?" Seth asked.

Arthur took out the map that was given to him by the security guard earlier and said, "Oh, I want to go to the National Museum of Crime and Punishment. It's only a few blocks from here."

They all agreed and spent the next few hours as tourists.

CHAPTER 30

Ford's Theater initially held almost 600 occupants, but since the renovation that number had been cut in half. The auction took place on the main stage, and about seventy-five percent of the floor-level seats were filled up. Seth and Madison were the youngest in the crowd, as most people were in their fifties and sixties. Rich, lush red carpet softened their step as they found seats on the left-hand side of the stage. Ironically, they had a clear view of Lincoln's box on the other side of the theater. Flags draped the outside of the box and a framed picture of George Washington hung beneath the balcony. The seats resembled those at a movie theater and they were comfortable after a long day on their feet.

After they had handed in their tickets they were given four numbered paddles for bidding purposes. Seth informed the woman that they only needed one so he returned them. On his paddle was written the number 212 in large black numerals. He was going to do the bidding only if Arthur agreed on the price. They estimated that the door might go for anywhere between ten and fifteen thousand dollars. After all, it *was* only a door.

The auctioneer got settled onstage and a curtain was drawn back from the stage so that the auctioned items could be revealed. The auctioneer was a young man with red hair. He wore a black suit and white gloves. A few others, both men and women, were scattered about the stage arranging the items and showcasing them for the spectators.

The auctioneer spent the better part of the first hour selling things that they had no interest in. This, of course, caused both Willie and Arthur to nod off; sometimes waking up when there was brief applause. The man was fast, just like on TV, Seth thought. Not as fast as some he'd seen, but he still got the job done. There was a lot of artwork being sold. The Theater shuffled artwork in and out every six months so as to keep the place fresh and to give artists a chance at selling their work at the auction. There were some historical pieces but nothing that related to Lincoln until the man came to the velvet rope.

"This here ladies and gentlemen is an eight foot velvet rope that marked the entrance to President Abraham Lincoln's private box which you see above us." He raised his left arm, indicating the location of the box. "Just imagine how many times Mr. President and his wife laid their hands upon this very rope."

A man also dressed in black and wearing white gloves, slowly walked back and forth on the stage, the velvet rope laid over his arms.

"We shall start the bidding at one thousand dollars," he began. "Do I hear one thousand?"

A paddle went up in the front row. Seth followed the action. The auctioneer moved in increments of five hundred dollars until it came down to two men at the eight thousand dollar mark.

"Do we have eight thousand?" the man on stage said into the microphone. "Eight thousand, eight thousand." His eyes scanned the room. "Eight thousand, going once…going twice….sold to one eight six for seven thousand five hundred." The man concluded the bidding with a smack of the gavel he was holding.

The applause was greater this time.

"Next up on the list, we have the door to President Abraham Lincoln's private box which you see above us. He extended his arm like before and all one hundred pairs of eyes followed him once again to the item on display. This time two men held the door, both donning the white gloves. They held the white door upright with both hands, walked ten paces then put it down. This was then repeated for the entire length of the stage. It looked pretty beat up, even from this distance. Scuff marks and holes battered the narrow door.

"Ready son?" Arthur asked.

Seth leaned forward and gripped the paddle. "If that rope went for seventy-five hundred, we may be out of our league here."

"I told you not to worry about it," Arthur said.

This time the auctioneer began the bidding at twenty-five hundred and a few people jumped in right away. Seth had never been to an auction before but he knew the smart thing to do was not to bid up the price of the item you wanted to buy. It was best to wait on it, and then jump in. The door passed the five thousand mark and continued through ten thousand not five minutes later. There was a lull in the action so Seth stuck up his paddle.

"We have ten five, over here to my right, new bidder, ten five. Do we have eleven?"

The man who had taken it to ten hesitated but eventually put up his paddle. He and Seth went at it until twelve thousand five hundred. The man looked up at the auctioneer and slowly shook his head; he was not taking it to thirteen.

"Yes," Madison said softly. "Almost ours."

"Do we have thirteen, thirteen? Current bid is twelve five, do I hear thirteen? Going once…"

"Come on," Seth said under his breath.

"Going twice…"

Seth smiled as the man picked up the gavel and raised it six inches over the lectern.

"Sss….thirteen, we have thirteen, new bidder in the back number 214. Thirteen, do we have thirteen five?"

Seth heart sunk into his chest. Who had just topped his bid? He turned in his seat and stared into the cold, steel eyes of the Brit he encountered outside of Madison's house.

"What the?" he said softly, turning back in his chair. They'd been followed again, but how?

"Seth!" Madison said, elbowing him in the stomach.

Seth held up his paddle and continued the bidding. His thoughts had distracted him and he almost lost it.

He looked over at his granddad who only gave him thumbs up to continue the bidding. The man in the back came back over top of him, and Seth did the same. They topped eighteen thousand in mere seconds but the guy in the back was slowing down his bids. The red-haired woman next to him was on the phone and looking like she was pleading with someone on the other end.

Minutes later Seth held up his paddle at nineteen thousand five hundred. He looked over at his granddad who simply shrugged his shoulders. He turned back to see the woman close the phone and shake her head.

"Twenty, twenty, do I hear twenty?"

Seth and his bidding foe locked eyes and a smile crept across his face. He had won.

"Going once…going twice…sold to bidder 212. Congratulations."

The loudest applause of the night was for Seth who had just paid nineteen thousand five hundred for a door. But it wasn't just any door.

They settled up at the end of the auction using multiple credit cards. Arthur only had one and the limit was reached, so Willie used his, and Seth had put three thousand on his, with promises of a pay back. Arthur had no real revelation of why he wanted to spend the money or where it came from. He just insisted he would be the one footing the bill, stating, "I can't take it with me." Seth was worried the nineteen five would be all for naught if they found nothing.

After they signed their credit card statements, they had to discuss transportation and delivery of the door. Madison was so excited that she wanted to throw it in

Willie's pick-up and bring it back to his house, but the theater wouldn't allow any such delivery. They wanted to deliver it themselves, or pack it securely for them for the ride home. Seth, remembering his foes at the auction, knew they would be followed. If they were followed home or anywhere else, those people would take the door and their quest would be over. He had another idea.

He approached a nearby security guard and asked, "Do you have a room in the back that we could use for a brief period of time?"

The husky man in the red sport coat with bronze buckles looked at him in surprise.

Seth restated his question, "Sir, we just bought an item at the auction and would like to look at it in private before taking it home. Do you have a room where we can view this?"

The man nodded his head and told them to follow him.

He led them through a cavernous maze of rooms in the back of Ford's Theater. At one point Seth thought he was going down when he was actually going up. They arrived at a conference room and Seth instructed the guard to have the door brought to them there. He also put two twenty dollar bills in his hand and told the man to stand guard outside the door and keep it locked.

"Why?" the guard asked.

"Listen, we just paid twenty grand for this thing and I don't wanna be bothered while I check it out. Fair enough?"

The guard just nodded, took the two twenties and left them alone.

When the door closed there was excitement and anticipation in the room. It was windowless with an oak conference table in the center surrounded by what looked to be comfortable vinyl chairs, typically used in an office. In the back of the room there was another door and Seth went over to make sure it was locked. There was a pitcher of water on a side table with condensation oozing down its side. Little droplets of water clung to the glass, reminders of the ice that melted away. Madison went over and poured herself a glass as Seth spoke.

"We have to prepare ourselves that this may be another dead end so let's not get our hopes up too high."

Arthur collapsed into a chair. "Well, I just paid twenty grand for this door so it better be something."

They all sat around the table in silence for a few moments before there was a knock on the door. Seth rose from his chair and went to the door.

"Yes?" he said.

"I'm here with the door," came the response on the other side.

Seth twisted the brass knob and opened the door. The security guard from earlier was standing there with an outstretched arm, leading two other men into the room. They carried the door into the room, still with their white gloves on. The white paint was very faded, it was about seven feet in height and it was obviously heavy as the two men held their breath carrying it in. They leaned it against the nearest wall and soon left. Willie, Arthur and Madison joined Seth, approaching the door like it was a time bomb.

"So here it is," Willie said.

"Ladies and gentlemen," Arthur said, "the door to President Abraham Lincoln's private box at Ford's Theater."

Madison was the first to move toward the door, hands touching the wood ever so gently. She moved her hand down to the hole which at one time held the door knob. There were literally scratches and scuff marks on half the door.

"This is a piece of crap for twenty grand," Arthur said.

"It's a piece of history," Madison said.

Now everyone was touching it, running their fingers over the wood ever so gently as if touching a newborn child.

"What's this hole for?" Madison wondered out loud. About a third of the way into the middle and halfway up was a round hole, about the size of the bullet they saw earlier.

"Lincoln's security drilled that hole," Willie said. "That way, they could look in on the President without disturbing him."

Seth was busy studying the contours of the wood, looking for an opening like the one Madison spotted on the floor of the tomb at Mount Vernon. He flipped it over and did the same on the other side. There was no noticeable gap in which a secret compartment could hold a treasure.

"There's nothing here," Madison stated.

Seth ignored her and knelt down to examine the lower portion and felt the urge to agree with her but he didn't. He sat on the ground and said, "Pick it up."

Willie and Arthur grabbed the door on either side

and heaved the door into the air about six inches.

"Higher," Seth said, leaning over with his face inches from the floor. "Tilt it a little."

They did so that the door was about twenty degrees titled toward them.

Arthur struggled with the piece and said, "Hurry up, this thing is heavy."

Seth saw it at once.

"Bring it over to the table." He got up and helped the men take the door over to the conference table and carefully set it on the flat surface.

"Look," he said.

He pointed toward the bottom of the door. The grain on the bottom of the wood was worn, probably from all of the opening and closing over the years. The wood was thicker than most doors, about three inches. Two thirds of the way back towards the hinges, the grain was smoother to the touch and it was not the same color that encompassed the rest of the door. There was a small slit in the door that ran along the edge from front to back. He stuck his fingernail it its edge and tried to pull open what looked like a hidden compartment. He could not get it open. Madison brushed him aside and tried with her longer fingernails to no avail.

Willie reached into his pocket and produced his keychain, from which his tiny Swiss Army knife was dangling. "Never leave home without it," he said.

"Oh my gosh," Madison said in anticipation.

Willie flipped open the small knife and shoved it inside the small slit, wiggling it back and forth until it sunk into the wood. After several seconds, the piece of wood buckled and slid forward and out. Seth used his hand to grab the small piece and removed it.

"Geez," Madison said. "It couldn't be."

The hole in the bottom of the door was small but deep, extending the width of the door. Seth was the first to reach his fingers in and feel around. He was not disappointed in his efforts.

February 12th, 1865

Another snowstorm pelted the northeast overnight. It was a bad winter by all accounts, the snow being the most recent bad news. The wind pushed and pulled the snowdrifts in all directions. In some areas the whiteness climbed to four feet and in others just a smatter of inches. A nor'easter they call it, formed in the Atlantic north of Georgia and bringing its fury along the eastern seaboard from the Carolinas to Boston.

President Abraham Lincoln was unsure if he was going to get to the theater for *The Frozen Deep*, a Charles Dickens play. It was his birthday and he had dinner earlier than usual at the White House and proceeded the few miles to Ford's Theater in horse and buggy. He wanted to get to the theater early, he told his wife. He carried with him a black satchel and when his security detail offered to take it for him, he refused, preferring to carry it himself.

They walked into the theater and were greeted with polite handshakes and nods of the head. The President doffed his top hat and removed his coat. He told his wife to wait for him downstairs and he and his head security detail, Joseph Henry, headed up to his box, satchel in hand. As they reached the door to his private viewing box, he opened his case and handed Joseph a screwdriver and instructed him to remove the hinges on the door. Joseph was not alarmed at such an unusual request as he was informed earlier of his task.

After removing the door and placing it inside the box, Lincoln instructed Joseph to wait outside and said he would call him to replace the door in a few moments. Lincoln began chiseling away the bottom of the door with the tools he had brought with him. Soon the hole in the bottom was large enough for his intended purposes. He went to his case and removed the document that he cherished so much. The war was almost over, but Rebels were known to be just that, rebels. He could not trust keeping the document in the White House anymore. He read it once more and rolled it into a tight cylinder and placed it inside.

"This will do," Lincoln said.

He double-knotted a piece of twine around the parchment and placed it carefully inside. He finished by placing another piece of wood in its place and called Joseph to replace the door on its hinges.

Lincoln's secret was safe for now. As presidents before him had done, he planned to tell the next incoming president the secret that only he and the vice-president had shared and also of its whereabouts. Sadly, John Wilkes Booth did not allow that to happen.

CHAPTER 31

Kim nestled over to Vice President Jonathon Castle on the couch. This time, he had taken her to a hotel for fear of exposure. She had just finished satisfying the VP and they were watching CNN on the television when his phone rang. He expected another update from Kohler but it was not him on the other end.

"Bannister?" Castle asked.

"Yeah," came the voice on the other end. "Get your dick out of your hands."

He looked over at Kim and thought a sarcastic comment might be in order but he passed.

"What's going on?" the VP replied.

"What's going on is that your little friends are at Ford's Theater."

"They're still at Ford's Theater?" the VP said, rising from the clutches of Kim and walking toward the window. He was dressed only in a t-shirt and boxer shorts. The hair that was left on his head was strewn about. "Why?"

"They bought the damn door to Lincoln's box. I couldn't justify spending twenty grand on something so we let them have it. Doesn't matter really, we'll take it from them soon enough."

"Did they find anything?"

"Don't know for sure," Bannister responded. "My guys are mulling about in the hallway and they are in the back."

"Take them now," Castle stated.

Kim had risen from the couch as well and moved to the kitchen portion of the suite. She opened the mini bar and looked at the assortment of beverages inside. She had on just a t-shirt as her clothes were scattered around the floor. Her fleshy body bent down and removed a clear mini bottle of vodka. She twisted the cap and breathed it in. Kim scrunched up her nose and shook her head violently like a baby tasting canned squash for the first time. She poured the contents into a glass and filled the remainder with a can of tomato juice from the small refrigerator.

"Are you sure?" Banister asked.

"They've got it," Castle responded.

"Now how do you know that?"

"I don't but if they found the document, they could destroy it or worse."

Castle felt Bannister's hesitation on the other end. "There could be consequences," Bannister stated.

"That's my business," Castle said. "Just tell them to get back there and see what they've found."

They bid their goodbyes and Castle moved back to the couch. Kim followed and handed him a small glass of Tanqueray on the rocks. She nestled up to him and they sipped their drinks in silence.

Ricky Winters never even put up a fight. That was his nature of course, never the one to go and pick a fight. On the school bus he tended to sit toward the front, away from the troublemakers. One teacher classified him as “self-sufficient,” which was true in a sense. He cared about one person, himself. So when two men and a woman came down the hallway toward him, he didn’t earn his forty bucks from the man inside the room.

They came at him quickly. Ricky was caught off guard and barely deflected the first punch. He crouched low and was broadsided by another hit to the back of the head. Soon thereafter he felt a pinch in his neck and all mobility ceased and he collapsed to the floor.

“Security guards, huh.” Evan said. He moved the body of Ricky Winters away from the door and Chloe and Max stepped forward.

The woman with the red hair reached forward and slowly twisted the doorknob. Locked. She looked up and down the door to determine its strength and decided she could do it. Chloe turned to the two men and nodded. She stepped back and raised her right leg into position. The gray leather boot extended forcefully and the door to the conference room crashed open.

Seth pulled out the rolled piece of paper and held it for all of them to see. “Here it is,” he said.

The three others stepped closer and they all reached out to touch it. It was about ten inches in length and tied with a piece of twine. The paper was yellow and brown and looked as old as they had hoped. In the quiet of the room they heard the muffled sound of a struggle outside the door and a thud as Ricky Winters dropped to the carpet.

Panic set in.

They had been discovered. They ran to the back of the conference room, unlocked and opened the door, and they all rushed through it.

Seth was the last to exit when the front door came crashing inward. He saw the door splinter when it thrust open, hanging by only the top hinge. The red-haired woman was the first set of eyes to see them. She quickly rushed in, followed by the two men.

Seth closed the door behind him. He looked around and discovered they were in the back of the theater where there were ladders, lights and every piece of equipment needed to effectively run a theater. He gave Madison the scroll to put in her purse and pushed them ahead. They had just turned the corner into a hallway when Seth heard the door open behind them.

"Hurry, go," Seth said, urging them along.

They picked up the pace and made their way down the hall. There were doors every ten feet on their left hand side. He passed everyone and led them through the labyrinth of halls until they came to a fork. They went right. The next fork he went left. He turned his head slightly and Willie and Arthur were a few paces behind Madison. He had to get them out of there.

The hallway came to an end, and there was a door

with a red "exit" sign overhead. He glanced at the sign next to the door that indicated that the alarm would sound if opened. Ignoring the warning, he burst through the door and no alarm sounded. The others followed.

They were outside.

It took a minute for Seth to get his bearings. They were in front of the theater but came out one building down on the same side. Everyone tried to catch their breath, but he knew they couldn't stand around and wait for the Brits to barge through the door.

"Now what?" Madison asked.

"We have to move," he replied.

"Okay, back to the truck," Willie said.

They turned to head to the parking garage and were met by Secret Service Agent Kohler.

"Hello folks," he said.

No one moved. They turned to leave, and Kohler opened his coat revealing his shoulder holster that housed his SIG Sauer P229 pistol. This was the second gun they'd seen up close that day. The similarities ended with the fact that they were both guns. Kohler's was thick and black and Seth did not want to test its accuracy or firepower. His head turned as a dark SUV abruptly pulled around the corner and stopped on the street in front of them.

"Get in," Kohler said, nodding toward the truck.

"All of us?" Seth asked. "Can't you just take me?"

"All of you," he replied. Kohler opened the front passenger door and pushed Seth inside. He closed the door and opened the back door and escorted Madison into the third row of seats and he followed Willie and

Arthur into the second row. He closed the door and told Pierce to go. Once the vehicle was in motion Seth turned and looked back at the Theater. The three Brits exited the building and looked around, wondering where their prey had gone.

In 1933 President Roosevelt had an indoor swimming pool built for his polio therapy. Unfortunately, Nixon had covered the pool and built a press room above it. Once Gerald Ford took over, he constructed an outdoor heated swimming pool which he tried to use on a daily basis, once holding a press conference as he did his laps.

President Richard Bowe, an avid swimmer, did his freestyle laps at a leisurely pace late in the evening. Earlier, he received another call from his source and sent his best man, Brent, over to Ford's Theater. Pacing in his office did him no good so he came out there to get a little exercise under the careful watch of four Secret Service agents.

As he made it to the end of a lap and turned to swim the other way, he heard his phone ring and signaled to the closest agent to bring it to him. He didn't bother checking caller id because very few had this number.

"Yes," he said.

"Mr. President," Brent said on the other end.

"Yes, go ahead Brent." The President waded into the middle of the pool out of earshot from the other agents.

"I parked outside and waited. I watched Kohler and Pierce do the same. I didn't see anyone for a while but then four people came out of the theater right into the hands of Agent Kohler."

"Who were they?" Bowe asked.

"I don't know, sir. Two old guys, a young woman and a young man. They were only outside for a second before Kohler escorted them into his SUV, which I assume Pierce was driving."

"Where are you now?"

"I'm following them," Brent replied.

The President contemplated his next move. He had to stay as far away from this as possible, but he also had to know what was going on.

"You need assistance?" the President asked.

"I'm not sure, sir. I don't know what we're up against besides Kohler and Pierce. Wait, it looks like they just pulled into the Madison Hotel on fifteenth."

"Okay, stay with them. I'll send some backup. Once they arrive, go in and try and find what room they're in."

"Okay sir, I'll keep you posted."

They ended the call and the President got out of the pool and toweled off. He said something to a couple of agents and they radioed into their command. Within seconds, the reinforcements arrived and three agents took off for the parking lot. He wanted to shower and crawl into bed, but he had a feeling that this could be a long night.

Chris Blewitt

CHAPTER 32

The Madison Hotel was lit up like a Christmas tree as most of the rooms were occupied with business travelers from all over the world who worked tirelessly through the night. The SUV pulled into the parking garage, parked, and the six people got into an elevator and headed to the twelfth floor, the highest floor in the hotel. Pierce led the way down the hall and stopped at room 1211 to insert his keycard and open the door. Not exactly a suite but bigger than a standard room, Arthur whistled as he imagined the room costing a couple hundred dollars a night.

"So this is where my taxes go, eh?" he said.

"Sit down," Kohler said, motioning them into the portion of the room that had two leather chairs and a soft couch made from some type of grainy white fabric. Arthur chose the couch, Willie and Madison the chairs and Seth decided to stand.

"What do you want?" Seth asked.

Kohler looked over at Pierce who was leaning against the wall, twirling a toothpick in his mouth. "You still don't get it, do you?"

"Get what?" Seth replied.

"I'm sick of playing games," Kohler said. "Hand it over."

Seth extended both arms and said, "What?"

Kohler walked over to Seth and punched him in the face. "Search him," he said to Pierce.

After a few tense moments of silence, Pierce walked over and just like at Mount Vernon, Seth was searched from head to toe. He rubbed his cheek as he was patted down and gingerly touched his nose to check for blood, but didn't find any.

"Clean," Pierce said to Kohler.

"Search 'em all while I use the phone," Kohler said.

"Touch me and I scream rape," Madison said. Madison made an effort to clutch her small beige purse even tighter. They didn't have to search her to find the scroll, just her purse.

Kohler walked out of the room as Pierce had Willie and Arthur stand up. Seth looked over at Madison. This was their chance if they wanted to make a run for it. She didn't make eye contact. Her eyes were on her purse, and for good reason. Seth watched as Pierce searched the two men from top to bottom. Coats, pants pockets, shirttails, shoes, anything that could hide something, Pierce searched it.

Kohler walked back after using the phone in the other room. "Anything?" he asked.

Pierce nodded his head. "Must be the girl."

Madison opened her mouth to scream when the door to the room opened.

Brent McCarthy sat in the SUV across the street from the Madison Hotel when a small sedan raced past the hotel, abruptly turned the corner and slammed down the ramp into the parking garage. He knew his reinforcements were seconds behind him so he radioed ahead and told them he was going into the garage.

He steered his car down the ramp cautiously but aggressively, scanning left and right for the headlights of the car that just entered. He found it three lanes away. It parked and turned its lights off. He found a spot and turned his lights off as well, but keeping the engine running. The parking garage was about half full and there were no other pedestrians walking throughout the various floors that he could see. He crouched low but kept his eyes on the car.

First out of the passenger seat was a woman with deep red hair tucked into her dark green jacket. Two men quickly followed out of the driver's side, front and backseat. They shut the doors, looked around and moved toward the elevators. They had guns.

Brent waited until they were in the elevator and then killed the engine and raised his transmitter to his lips and spoke. "McCarthy here. Three suspicious subjects just got out of a late model sedan at the Madison. Two male, one female. How far out?"

"Approaching now, McCarthy," came the voice in his ear. "Where are you?"

Brent directed them down the ramp and the other SUV parked a few spaces away from them. Three men got out of the other Lincoln, two black, one white, all of similar build, tall with thick shoulders and compact legs. They removed their ties, threw them in the truck and walked over to Brent.

"What's the status here McCarthy?" the taller of the two black men had asked.

"We got four unknowns captured or detained by agents Kohler and Pierce of Vice-President Castle's detail inside. Then, these three unknowns that just showed up unexpectedly."

"Driving over here, we called the front desk, identified ourselves and got the room number they're in, 1211. There is no one in room 1209 and an unknown registrar in 1213."

"What do you mean, unknown in 1213?" McCarthy asked.

"Exactly that. Someone who doesn't want to be identified. Diplomat, foreign personnel, whatever. Howell," he said to the man next to him, "go down and get a key for 1209 and 1211. Meet us in the north stairwell on the twelfth floor."

The second black man took one set of stairs down, and the other three men took the nine flights of stairs up. They'd been taught it was better not to use an elevator and trap yourself in. When they reached the top of the concrete stairwell, the men were winded but not gasping for breath. Used to running and walking alongside motorcades, they were in fairly decent shape. They withdrew their German-made pistols and waited in formation. Two men were positioned on the opening side of the door along the wall and Brent was stationed a few feet away on the second step of the stairwell.

Behind them, down the stairs, they heard the sound of footsteps getting closer. Brent leaned his head between the rails and peered down at the bald black head of Agent Howell. He held up two keycards. A moment later he arrived and they opened the door to the twelfth floor. Howell was the first one through and the others followed, moving in typical formation, each covering another's back as they made their way forward. They stopped at room 1209. Agent Howell slipped the keycard in and they entered.

When the door closed they heard loud voices in the room next to them.

Madison was shocked to see the face of the red-haired woman in the doorway of the hotel room. Kohler and Pierce would be the first to admit that they were surprised as well.

"What are you doing here?" Kohler asked.

Chloe entered the room followed by Max and Evan. They moved through the room admiring their surroundings.

"Nice place you got here," Max said.

"I asked you a question. We can handle it," Kohler stated.

Pierce decided to goad the three Brits and said, "Seems like you all lost them at the theater, eh? Can't handle two old men and two kids?"

Evan chided back, "How's the nose?"

"Go to hell," Pierce said. He moved toward the door and Kohler didn't attempt to stop him. "Wanna go right now you bastard?"

"Be my bloody pleasure," Evan said. He started to remove his jacket and this time was stopped by Max.

"Don't be a bloody arse. You want someone to call security or better yet the cops? Handle it after we're done here." He turned to Kohler and asked, "You find anything yet?"

"Not yet. We searched all but the girl."

"Well," Max said smiling and turning towards Madison. "This could be fun."

"Touch me and I scream rape," Madison said again. Her eyes floated about the five intruders. She watched the red-haired girl slide around behind the two Americans.

"Oh, a tough one, is ya?" Max replied. "You know what happens to tough girls, don't ya?" He waited for a reply but none came. "They get what they ask for." He nodded and said, "Chloe."

Before Madison could turn her head to see the woman, she was on her. She grabbed hold of the back of her hair from behind and threw her down on the couch. Madison watched as Seth yelled something, made a move toward her and was caught from behind by one of the Brits. Chloe jumped on her waist, straddling her and pinched her nose as tight as she could. Madison's only thought now was for her survival.

Her nose burned, and she could feel the cartilage inside being twisted and smashed as the woman squeezed tighter and twisted upwards at an angle.

Madison flailed her hands wildly striking the woman but having no effect. She reached up and found the flesh on her face and dug in with all her strength.

Chloe screamed in anger as a half dozen fingernails slashed across her face causing an extraordinary amount of pain. She let go of Madison's nose and clutched her face. She pulled back and saw crimson traces of blood on both hands.

"You bitch," Chloe yelled. She pulled back her right arm and before Madison could defend herself, struck her in the side of the head near her ear.

Madison put a hand up to her ear and felt her head ringing in pain. She looked at the seven men just standing there and her vision blurred. She felt hands combing her body, reaching into pockets, into the front of her pants, the back, taking off her shoes. Then the woman they called Chloe found her purse under her right leg and pulled it out.

Once again the door opened.

CHAPTER 33

Being a Secret Service agent had a lot of responsibility tied to it. You were either part of the US Treasury investigating counterfeit money or bonds or you were in charge of protecting former and current national leaders and their families. One thing they were not willing to do was kill a fellow agent unless their life was in danger. They always carried rubber bullets and McCarthy suggested that three of them switch out their guns and he and Howell would stay loaded with the .357 cartridge.

They moved swiftly out of room 1209 and down the hall to the next door on their left. Using the same formation they used in the hallway, Howell slowly slipped the keycard in the lock and twisted the handle. He held up a hand showing all five fingers. He quickly pulled down his digits.

Four

Three

Two

One

The door opened and all hell broke loose.

They weren't sure what they would encounter. Would it just be Kohler and Pierce or would it be the other three unknowns as well? As soon as they entered with weapons raised, they knew they were outnumbered, four against five. Fortunately, they were the ones with the element of surprise and they caught the others off guard.

Closest to the door were the two men that arrived late to the hotel with the girl. Howell was the first in and saw that they were not in any eminent danger of a firearm. He was through the door and on Max in seconds. He brought his foot up and caught him square in the groin. As soon as Max doubled over, Howell pressed his two hands together with the gun hidden and raised them violently, crashing into the man's face. He went down.

At the same time Howell's partner, Franklin, was on Evan. Although he was outweighed by at least thirty pounds, Franklin was much quicker. After his initial blow to the ribcage, Evan threw a wild punch that landed on Franklin's shoulder. It did have some force behind it but it landed in the bulk of muscle mass. Franklin whirled left and was behind Evan and threw a hard right in the side of his head. He grabbed the back of Evan's head and threw him down, right into his waiting knee.

There were screams and yelling and "stop" and "wait" for the better part of a minute as chaos reigned inside the hotel suite. Two men were down and Kohler and Pierce had a look of shock and resignation on their faces. They backed up and allowed the four agents from the Presidential detail to enter the room.

Chloe, on the other hand, didn't get off Madison. She was still straddling her and had now tucked her arms beneath her legs. Her left hand was holding the closed purse, and her right hand was down on the couch. Chloe moved the right hand backward. Her hand crept along her leg like a spider on its web. She watched as the men yelled back and forth at each other trying to sort things out. Chloe pulled up her pant leg ever so slightly. Madison, still in a daze saw the glint of steel peek out from her black boot.

Chloe turned toward the men and a smile drizzled across her mouth. She put a finger into the loop of the trigger and dragged the gun out of her boot. It was just about out when Madison came to and said, "Who'd you call bitch?"

A confused Chloe turned her head, gun fully in her hand. Madison bucked the back of her legs up at the same time constricting her abdominals and crouching forward. Chloe rose forward on Madison's legs just as Madison came up. Madison swiftly steered her forehead perfectly into Chloe's nose and heard the crunch of bone on bone. Both women went back and Chloe fell off Madison onto the floor and dropped the gun.

Seth scrambled for the gun.

"Put that gun down!" yelled one of the men that had just saved his life.

It was the first time he had held a real gun and it only lasted all of three seconds as he quickly dropped it to the floor.

No more questions were asked, and it was clear who was in charge. Agents Abbott and Costello, as Seth knew them, were left standing in the suite staring at them as they walked out the hotel door. The new agents didn't ask Seth who they were or what they were doing there. They had brought Kohler and Pierce into an adjoining bedroom for a few moments then came out and told Seth and Madison to follow them. The Brits came back from their slumber and waited while the local DC police arrived, Kohler and Pierce standing guard.

They were escorted out to the parking garage and placed in separate SUV's. Howell and Franklin rode in one with Willie and Arthur in the back seat. Brent took the other agent and placed Seth and Madison in their backseat.

"Where are we going?" Madison asked. She was scrunching her nose back and forth trying to get feeling back in. Seth rubbed his cheek, feeling the small bump that would probably be larger by morning.

Brent looked over at his partner and didn't reply.

"Where do you think we're going?" Madison said to Seth.

He shrugged his shoulders. "Beats me and I don't care. It's gotta be safer than with those other guys." His eyes gazed toward her purse and he whispered, "You still…?"

She unzipped the purse, looked inside, and quickly

zipped it back up. She nodded at him. She thought about taking it out and reading it but knew the men in front would confiscate it. Seth turned in his seat to make sure the other truck was following them and it was. A few miles later he looked out the tinted windows and his surroundings looked familiar.

The truck stopped at a gate for a few moments and they were led inside the grounds of the White House.

CHAPTER 34

They were in awe as they made their way through the hallways of the 132-room mansion. No one could guess it was approaching midnight as staff members walked swiftly throughout the maze of corridors. Seth and the others gazed every which way trying to take in as much as possible. Two agents walked in front and two in the rear, every so often talking softly to their wrist. They went into an elevator and then down some stairs and came upon a hallway deserted except for one guard standing outside a door.

The agents walked to the man, nodded their heads and he stepped aside. He knocked once and led the way in, followed by Seth, Madison, Willie, and Arthur.

The smack of a billiard ball was the first thing that Seth heard as the door was closed behind him and the first agent had left the room. He looked around the room and saw a man with his back to them stand up after being crouched low along a red felt billiards table.

He was wearing a white shirt neatly tucked into dark blue trousers. His sleeves were rolled up and he had no tie on.

"Mr. President," Seth exclaimed.

"Hi ya folks, Richard Bowe, please come in." He set the pool cue on the table and walked toward them. He walked over to the bar in the corner and offered them a drink. It had been a long day and they all obliged.

"Shouldn't you have a servant doing that?" Arthur asked.

The President chuckled. "Just because I'm President, doesn't mean I can't put ice in a glass and pour something over it." He handed two bourbons to Willie and Arthur and went to the small black refrigerator in the corner to retrieve three beers for Seth, Madison and himself. It was a local beer from Capitol City Brewery.

There were pictures throughout the room, most with the current President shaking hands with movie stars, diplomats, and even a few sports stars. A few chairs were placed throughout the room along with waist high cabinets and drawers. Three windows were along the west wall, their drapes closed and there were two doors in the back, also closed.

"So, first I want to apologize for all you went through these past few days. I, myself, just found out about it today. I want to ask you something and I want an honest answer. Did you find anything at the auction in Lincoln's door?"

They all looked at each other and Seth decided whom better to trust than the President. "Yes, sir we have."

"Damn, of all the places to look. How'd you come to find it there?" he asked.

They spent the next twenty minutes going over their discovery of the safety deposit box with Washington's journal, then Betsy Ross, Valley Forge, Mount Vernon and finally Ford's Theater.

"I need to have it," the President said, no denying the threat in his tone. "I appreciate what you have done, but I cannot let you leave here with it."

They didn't know what to do. It was the President after all. Seth spoke again. "Tell us about it."

"You haven't read it yet?" Bowe asked.

"Ah, no," he replied.

"Huh, I could just take it from you and you'd never know, would ya?" He drank some more of his beer and changed his mind. "I guess I owe you that much. But if one word leaves this room, I'll know where it came from, and your lives will never be the same, is that understood?"

They all nodded and walked over to the stools by the bar and had a seat. The President moved behind the bar like he was the barkeep. He made some more drinks in silence, slid a few beers across the bar and asked a question. "May I see it?"

The four of them exchanged glances, but Madison did not hesitate. This *was* the President. She unzipped her purse, reached in and pulled out the scroll and handed it over. The President accepted the offering and gingerly massaged the outside of the scroll with both hands.

"Finally," he began.

Now bound and gagged, Kohler and Pierce struggled to free themselves when the door opened and the Vice President walked in. It was just moments before that they were evaluating the situation that they had gotten themselves into. In the blink of an eye, four of their own agents burst through the door, took down the combatants from Great Britain and stole their hostages. There was nothing they could have done. What were they going to do, throw down with their co-workers? Shoot them? This was a delicate mission they were on and they failed.

After the agents had taken the hostages away, the Brits regained their composure. Kohler watched as they stammered around, cursing loudly. They went into the bathroom and got towels to wipe the blood from their wounds. Kohler almost smiled. They got their asses kicked. He was sure Pierce enjoyed it too. They were in the bathroom for a long time. He had grabbed Pierce by the arm and headed over to the half open door. Before he was even able to stick his head in and ask what they were doing, he was struck in the face.

Max, Evan and Chloe had come charging out of the bathroom as Kohler and Pierce tried to piece together what was going on. It was over quickly. Pierce was one on one with Evan and they traded punches for a few moments. Max and Chloe finished Kohler rather quickly and once he was down, helped Evan with Pierce. In less than three minutes they were tied together in bed sheets and pillow cases. They started on their knees with their backs to each other and their wrists secured but now they were on the floor, struggling to breathe.

"What the—" Castle asked, walking in and closing the door behind them. He went over to Kohler first and pulled the white pillow case down that was tied around his mouth.

Kohler inhaled deeply a few times before saying, "Sorry sir, they ambushed us."

"Who?" Castle asked. He untied Pierce's gag and then moved down to the sheets that were tightly bounding their wrists.

"The freakin' Brits," Kohler said. "They're gone. Said they didn't wanna be around when the cops showed up. We gotta move."

"Where the hell's the kid, the girl, the old guys?" Castle said sharply.

"Gone."

"Whadaya mean gone?" He finished freeing them and he stood back as they got to their feet and stretched their limbs.

"Sir, we gotta problem."

Castle waited for his right hand man to finish the sentence. A problem was never good to have, especially if you were the Vice President of the United States of America.

"The President knows," Kohler stated. He paused and watched the blood drain out of his boss' ashen face. "His men were here just a bit ago. They'd beaten the crap out of the Brits and took the hostages."

Castle ran his hand through the remaining strands of hair on his head. "And the document?"

Kohler shook his head.

CHAPTER 35

They were tired, but their attention was focused solely on the leader of the free world as he took a swig from his beer. The four of them drank copious amounts of their preferred drink and the President leaned in close with both hands on the bar, the scroll sitting between them.

"So this is it," President Bowe began. "This is what has been missing all this time. In all respects it didn't really matter that you found it. It just mattered that it didn't fall into the wrong hands." He picked up the scroll and pulled the string that enclosed the parchment. He unraveled it and read it to himself. "Yep, this is it all right." He placed it back on the bar.

Arthur made a move to grab it, but Bowe was quicker and snatched it from his grasp.

"Ah, this won't make much sense to you yet," he said. "Let me ask you a question sir," he said, looking at Arthur. "We're fighting a war right now, correct?"

Arthur didn't quite know what to say and looked at the others for the correct answer. Madison was the first to speak up and she said, "Afghanistan?"

The President nodded and replied, "Any others?"

Madison continued, "Iraq."

"Keep going."

After those two countries she didn't have anything else to add and looked to the others for assistance. Willie came to her rescue. "Korea."

The President nodded his head, "Yep, all of you are correct. There are even more…" he made imaginary quotations with his fingers in the air, "…engagements that I'm not even going to talk about. The point is, are we doing this alone? No, we have help from other nations. Who has helped us every step of the way?"

The President didn't let them respond and he continued. "Tony Blair got so much shit in his own country for allowing his countrymen to be killed for what they considered an illegal war during the first Iraqi War. Who was with us every step of the way in World War One, World War Two?" He outstretched his arms and was theatrical with his presentation. "Great Britain, England, the U.K., whatever you wanna call it is our best friend. America's best friend. You think we would invade Iraq without their blessing or support? Well, maybe we would, but the point is, they agree with whatever decisions we make. 'Want a new oil well in the Atlantic?' Sure, go right ahead. 'Can we build a military base in Northern England?' We'll hold your hand as you do it."

Seth took a swallow of his beer and thought about the President's questions and had no idea where he was going with this. *What did all this have to do with that piece of paper from two centuries ago?*

"Let's go back a bit," the President said. "Ever hear of the War of 1861?"

No one answered and their brows furrowed, trying to recollect their high school history classes. Finally, Willie spoke, "The Civil War?"

"No, that was a war within the States. I'm talking about the War of 1861. Nobody?" the President asked. "Of course not, it never existed. The reason being, this little piece of paper!" He dramatically picked up the scroll and held it over his head. "God, it feels good to finally tell people about this. But remember," he lowered his voice, "this goes nowhere." He picked up his own beer, took a drink and continued his story in a monotone voice. "In 1861 the Civil War broke out and President Lincoln made a tough decision. He had to finance the War and what better way to do it, than with his own people. Congress passed the first legal income tax bill in order to fund the war. Guess how much?"

The four people sitting across from him threw out their guesses ranging from twenty percent to seventy-five percent.

"Three percent," the President stated. "Yep, three percent income tax if you made over eight hundred dollars a year and five percent if you made over ten thousand, which was rare at the time."

"So that's why you take my money every paycheck," Madison said.

"Well, yes. You are lucky right now. There was a time when the maximum tax rate was ninety percent! Yes, ninety percent of your income was taken to fund the government due to a war or the Depression. That number has fluctuated along the way, and currently we sit in the mid to high thirties for your highest income bracket. Three percent seems like nothing, but if you only made eight hundred bucks a year, that was significant."

"Mr. President," Arthur said, "this is all very fascinating, but what does this have to do with anything and when are you going to let us read what's on that paper?"

The President smiled. He took a sip of his own drink and allowed the silence in the room to fester. He took his hands off the paper and pushed it across the bar. "Go right ahead."

February 13th, 1778

General George Washington was not caught off guard when the men wearing red entered the tent. He had left the warmth of his Quarters moments before when word arrived that the men were approaching fast on horseback, but without their cavalry; they were alone. He had met two of them before, but now the commander himself was inside. He and four British military men were the only ones in the tent.

"General Washington these are the terms we agreed upon, as did the King. We will continue the war as agreed upon and slowly withdraw our troops in the coming months and years. Those British soldiers who wish to stay in America will be subject to hanging for treason."

The General contemplated the decision. He moved past the men and toward the open flaps blowing in the harsh winter wind. He looked at the snow covered hills, the men scurrying back and forth from the nearby forest gathering wood for the night's fire. They were bruised and battered.

It was cold outside.

The General was far from defeated, but his purpose had been served. The Declaration of Independence was signed eighteen months ago and it was time for the war to end. He walked back inside and the Commander of the British Army brought out two scrolls and a quill for him to sign. He knew the offer. He'd seen it before but decided to read it over. He came to the last paragraph and read aloud:

"In return for a complete withdrawal of troops from the American mainland and complete freedom from her Royal Kingdom of Great Britain, I set forth the following precedent to be carried out by the government of the new United States of America; Starting on January 1, 1780, and each and every year moving forward on this date, the government of the United States of America will exchange one percent of their tariffs and taxes to the British Empire in a monetary denomination to be determined each year. Signed, King George III of England, Signed, General Commander of the United States Army, George Washington."

General George Washington of the Continental Army signed both papers.

CHAPTER 36

Seth tried to sum it up for himself. "So, Washington promised Britain one percent of tariffs and taxes in exchange for them leaving the country."

The President shrugged. "Pretty much."

"What's a tariff?" Madison asked.

Willie responded, "A tariff was a tax on all imported goods from other nations. So, Washington said that any dues collected from the import of goods from other nations, Britain would get one percent."

"Correct," the President stated.

"Wow," Seth said. "That's a lot of money."

"Not really, not then," the President replied. "They probably paid the Brits around forty thousand dollars a year in those days. It got interesting in 1861 when Lincoln made income tax a law."

"The war of 1861," Willie said.

"Yes, but it never happened," the President said. "When Lincoln proposed the income tax law, Britain got word of it and they were licking their chops. Lincoln refused to pay Britain the one percent on the new tax. The Prime Minister of Britain then prepared to invade America, hence The War of 1861. Lincoln already had the Civil War brewing. The nation would have been destroyed completely if he had to fight two wars. So he gave in and paid the Brits one percent of the new income tax. Hence, no War of 1861."

Arthur looked the President in the eye. "You're serious. And this is still…"

Everyone took their eyes off the scroll and noticed the stare down between Arthur and the President.

"It's true," the President said, "and we still pay them one percent."

Everyone gasped at the thought and you could see the whites of their eyes as they expanded.

This time Arthur summed it up for them. "So Great Britain gets one percent of our income taxes every year."

The President nodded. "As well as one percent of all imported goods taxes, or tariffs, if you will. In exchange, we get their approval and support for every global war, every time we invade a country, every time we require any support whatsoever, no matter what the circumstances, the economy, crime, drug wars, oil spills, stock market plunges, the recession, housing costs, education, everything, the Brits are there for us."

"Wow," Seth said.

"Wow is right," Madison agreed.

A thought came to Arthur, "How much is one percent?"

This time the President picked up his drink and

moved from behind the bar. He took a long swallow and kept his back to them before he said, "Last year we collected two point seven trillion dollars in personal income tax."

"That's trillion with a T?" a shocked Seth asked.

"Correct."

"So one percent is…?" Seth wondered aloud.

"Twenty-seven billion dollars," Willie responded.

Arthur whistled and started to chuckle. "Holy shit, that's a lot of money to give away. What about the tariffs collected?"

"Much smaller," the President responded, "we pay them only about two-hundred and fifty million each year."

Arthur cursed again.

"No wonder you want us to keep silent," Seth said. "Word gets out that the government is paying the Brits billions of dollars each year while the deficit is in the trillions, we're in a recession, people are losing their homes, unemployment rate is incredibly high, there's corporate fraud, Ponzi schemes, Freddie Mac, Fannie Mae, Jesus!'

"When you think about it, it's not that much money in the grand scheme of things," the President said, trying to calm the storm.

"The hell it's not," Arthur said. "You know what I made in my lifetime? I maxed out at forty-two thousand dollars a year. Now I'm in an old folk's home because I can't afford in-home care. Don't tell me twenty-seven billion dollars a year isn't a lot of money."

"I'm sorry, that's not what I meant. I mean that we give all kinds of money to other nations across the globe. We have to or they won't survive."

"Okay, enough already," Madison said, temporarily stopping the bitter argument. "I do have a question for you. Who were the men who have been following us? And who were the ones from England? And how did you find us?"

The President smiled and said, "Actually, that's three questions. The first one, those were secret service agents on the vice president's detail."

A hush came over the others as they contemplated the ramifications that lay ahead.

"The second group from England I assume is the deputy prime minister of England's men."

"What did they want with Washington's scroll?" Seth asked.

"Think about it. If they got their hands on this, I can kiss the presidency goodbye. I'd either be forced to resign for lying to the American public, or I would have no chance at re-election. I assume that's the same reason the Brits wanted it. There would be a public outcry if the British people found out that they were going to war for money. That they allowed the US to do anything they please for a kickback every year."

"Couldn't they just expose it anyway?" Madison asked.

"They could, but it would be denied. They'd have no proof. I hear they found the other copy in England. Without this one, we'll deny everything and call it a forgery. Also, folks, remember that if this got out, think about what it would do to our country's morale."

"What do you mean?" asked Madison.

"Our country was built by men who sacrificed their

lives in the Revolutionary War. George Washington, our Founding Father, basically bribed his way out of the war. Washington was a great man and an even greater president. Let's not tarnish his name for trying to do what was right and getting us out of the war."

Willie and Arthur moved over to the couch along the side wall and collapsed heavily into its supple leather. It had been a long couple of days and it was taking its effect on the old men. Seth and Madison stayed in their stools and followed the President's gaze as he stared upward, looking for answers.

"What are you going to do?" Seth asked.

"And how did you find us?" Madison asked.

Bowe interlaced his fingers and placed them behind his head, not looking at them. "First, you guys need to get some sleep. I'll arrange for a couple of spare bedrooms. There's no need for you to drive all the way back to wherever you were staying."

"We're going to sleep in the White House?" Arthur asked.

He nodded. "There are one hundred and thirty-two rooms here, I'm sure I can find a few bedrooms." He smiled and walked over to the couple on the barstools. "Thank you for everything." He shook their hands and picked up the scroll. "If this would've been found by the others, there would've been an uproar in the streets." He shook their hands and moved over to the men on the couch.

Willie stood up and shook the President's hand. Arthur stayed seated and spoke. "I think there should be some type of reward, don't you think?"

"Granddad!" Seth said from across the room.

"What? He wants us to keep our mouths shut, right? I could go to any news station and sell this information for fifty grand, maybe even a hundred."

The President looked down at the old man and said simply, "Listen, as an American, do this for your country. I'm asking this as a favor, please keep this quiet. I'll see what I can do about a reward. Thanks again."

Seth had a thought pop in his head and asked the President for a moment alone. They walked over to the corner and Seth whispered something into the President's ear. The President said something back and they shook hands.

CHAPTER 37

The sun poked and prodded its way through the sheer cloth that covered the two windows in his bedroom. It had been a restless sleep for the Vice President. He debated his course of action all night long. Deniability was his first option. He knew nothing, saw nothing, did nothing. The President couldn't prove anything. The second option was to beg forgiveness and apologize. Still deny that you wanted the presidency, but tell him you got a tip and you wanted to follow up on it.

But Jonathon Castle was not one to beg forgiveness of anyone, even from the President of the United States of America.

He was going to deny everything. Act just as shocked as the President appeared to be. *"Oh no! That secret can't get out!"* It was the only way to get through this in one piece. As long as the Brits stayed quiet, his role would be his little secret.

Castle got in his car and his driver was led to the

White House by another SUV filled with his Secret Service detail. He made sure that Kohler and Pierce called in sick for the day. They could certainly spoil this for him, but he doubted they would; their careers would be finished. The car drove to the White House and Castle made his way inside to his office, just down the hall from the Oval Office.

He made sure to get there early. He wanted the President to think that everything was okay just like the day before. Deniability.

After about an hour, busying himself with paperwork and checking emails, his intercom buzzed.

"Mr. Vice-President?" It was his secretary down the hall. "The President would like to see you in his office."

He knew it was coming. "Be right there," was all he could say.

He pulled his gray suit jacket off the coat stand in the corner, put it on and opened his door. Castle walked down the hall and tapped on the door to the Oval Office where a Secret Service agent was standing outside. The agent had red hair. Castle knew exactly who he was and more importantly where he had been the night before. The agent looked at Castle and curled his lips into a tiny grin as he opened the door.

Castle walked in and shut the door behind him.

Deniability.

The President was behind his desk and did not look up as the second-in-command walked into the room. "Sit down, Jon."

Castle came forward and sat on one of the couches in the center of the room. He wanted to talk, to shoot the shit, so to speak, and that was all. "Warming up out there," Castle said, trying to break the ice. "Summer will be here in no time. Nationals still suck though," he commented, referring to the city's baseball team.

The President ignored his small talk and got up from his chair and sat on the edge of his desk, facing the Vice-President. He crossed his arms and stared at him. "I want you to resign, effective immediately."

Castle was flabbergasted, and he stood up to defend himself. "What the hell are you talking about Richard!"

"Sit, down, Jon."

Castle sat back down on the couch and looked up at the President. "Are you out of your mind?"

"Let's not beat around the bush. You deliberately tried to run me out of office."

"And you have proof of this?"

The President simply nodded.

"Kohler and Pierce? Ha, they are loyal to me 'til the day I die."

"I've already had my speechwriter take care of your resignation speech. You'll deliver it at noon today in the briefing room. I will be by your side and support the decision."

"There's no way, Richard. I will do nothing of the kind."

The president ignored him and continued. "Health reasons, you'll say. Your doctor told you the stress on your heart is too much and you've asked me if you could step down. I agreed. It won't hurt my re-election chances and it won't hurt the party or the country. That is what's most important here, Jon."

"You're being irrational," Castle stated.

"Am I? Or am I just protecting this country from a scandal? I know you went after the document, Jon. You were so close you could taste it. You were in bed with Bannister and the Brits too. You had a whole plan to reveal this little secret to the American public and get me ousted from office. Weren't you?"

"You have no proof," Castle said.

The President pushed a button on his desk. "Come in."

Castle and Bowe both looked at the door to the Oval Office waiting for it to open. When it did, Castle's eyes cringed in fear. In walked Kim Bevin, the Vice-President's assistant. She directed her gaze away from the two men, shut the door behind her and walked into the middle of the room. In her hand, Castle could see a miniature tape recorder.

"You still need proof?" the President asked.

Castle leaned back in the chair and placed his hand on his forehead, rubbing the creases back and forth and trying to make sense of all this. He had been betrayed.

"Kim," he said.

She didn't reply. She simply curled her lips and gave a sarcastic "sorry" expression.

"How could you?"

The President spoke, "How could *you*, Jon?" He walked back around to his desk and sat down. "Resign. Go out with pride, some sense of dignity. Or, I play this little tape of your sexual exploits and let the media stalk you for the rest of your life." Without getting up, he extended his hand holding a sheet of paper. "Here. Your speech. See you at noon."

Castle slowly got up and walked to the President's

desk and took the sheet of paper. He walked back toward the door and paused in front of Kim. He wanted to slap her, shake some sense into her. He shook his head. "I can't believe you're doing this."

She didn't reply and he walked out the door.

"You owe me," Kim said.

"Believe me, I know."

She smiled at him and said, "How about your new Vice-President?"

He let out a slight laugh and said, "Let's start with something else first. I have another job for you."

CHAPTER 38

Sleeping in the White House did have its benefits and they took full advantage of them. They all slept in and met downstairs in the kitchen and ordered whatever they wanted for breakfast. They inquired about meeting the president but were denied access every time they asked. Seth thought that was odd. He thought maybe the president would want to see them again. Tie up any loose ends.

After breakfast, a new set of secret service agents escorted them through the halls and out the doors to an awaiting black town car. They piled in and were driven to the parking garage near Ford's Theater where Willie's truck was parked, before they paid twenty grand for Lincoln's door. Before they were kidnapped. Before they were rescued by the secret service. Before they met The President of the United States.

Willie drove them back to his house where Madison's car was parked. He and Arthur said their goodbyes and embraced like long lost soldier buddies, which they were. They promised to keep in touch, which was unlikely, but it was the right thing to say at the time. Madison made Seth drive home and she took the backseat, allowing Arthur to ride shotgun.

It was not until they rounded the Beltway and picked up Interstate 95 North that Arthur spoke. He smiled first and said, "We forgot the door."

"Shit!" Seth said, taking his foot off the accelerator. "I'll get off the next exit."

Arthur put his hand on Seth's leg. "Forget about it."

"What? We paid twenty grand for that, it's ours."

"What are you going to do with it? Leave it there. We got what we wanted. It's a piece of history. Let others enjoy it."

"Are you sure?"

"Let it go, son."

Madison agreed. "He's right, Seth. Let it go."

Seth reluctantly increased his speed and they drove on.

Just after twelve in the afternoon, every radio station they turned to was covering the surprise announcement that the vice president was stepping down due to health reasons.

They all knew that was a lie.

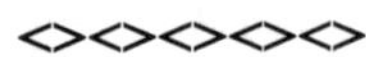

The following day Seth, was in his apartment cleaning up the mess made by the Brits. While he picked up the broken glass, the books strewn about, and the cushions from the couch, he heard a knock at the door. He put down the broom he was holding and opened the door to see a FedEx driver holding an envelope.

"Seth Layton?" the driver asked.

"Yeah."

"Please sign here," the driver said, handing him an electronic signature pad.

Seth signed, took the envelope and shut the door. He pulled the tear strip and pulled out a brown manila envelope secured with a metal clasp. He opened it and pulled out a few sheets of paper. The top sheet had the Presidential Seal at the top of it. He read the letter:

Mr. Seth Layton,

As we previously discussed, your cooperation in this matter has ended. We, the American people appreciate your hard work and that of your friends and family. I strenuously insist that you do not discuss this with anyone ever again. I do not need to remind you of the repercussions if something did happen to bring forth these events. Please remind your friends and family of the same.

Thanks again for all your fine efforts.

Sincerely,

President Richard Bowe.

PS. Please see enclosed as tokens of appreciation. I have also taken your request to heart and your grandfather has been placed at the top of the list at Johns Hopkins for a new liver. Please inform him and get him to the hospital no later than tomorrow.

Seth gawked at the signature of the President. He was in awe. *How did he know where he lived?* He is the President after all. He moved the letter to the side and lifted the next piece of paper.

It was a cashier's check made out to Arthur Layton in the sum of one million dollars.

"Holy shit," Seth said out loud.

The next piece was another check. This time made out to Willie for another million.

There were two pieces of paper left and he quickly shuffled them to find his check.

There wasn't one.

The remaining two letters looked identical. He read the first one:

To Whom it May Concern:

I hereby exempt Mr. Seth Layton, Social Security number 109-111-3530, from paying any state or federal income tax from this day forward until the day he dies. Please contact Kimberly Bevin, my personal assistant with any questions.

President Richard Bowe

He smiled to himself, flipped to the last sheet and saw the same note made out to Madison. "Wow," he said.

Not a million bucks, but it would do.

He grabbed his phone and was going to call Madison and his granddad. Instead, he picked up his car keys and headed out the door. This kind of news had to be delivered in person. Plus, it was another excuse to see Madison, and his granddad.

ACKNOWLEDGEMENTS

This book was very enjoyable to research and write. If you ever get a chance to tour the historic places as I did, don't hesitate. Standing in Ford's Theater and in front of Washington's tomb is a lot better than reading about it all these years. Thanks to all of the people who preserve and protect out National Landmarks.

The part about Washington having relations with a slave and fathering a child outside of marriage is in fact true. Well, that's for you to decide but visit www.westfordlegacy.com to learn more.

A big thanks goes out to Steve White, Tom Lill, and my mother-in-law, Dolly, for reading and editing this book before publication. Without their honest feedback and editing skills, I would have produced a much different and inferior final product. Cheryl Bradshaw, author of *The Sloane Monroe* series, edited this manuscript and I can't thank her enough. Thanks to Jason Merrick for a great cover. Jason also did the cover for *The Chemist* and I look forward to working with him again in the future.

I cannot forget my wife Katie for allowing me to spend endless nights in the basement re-reading and editing this book while she cared for our three children. Thanks for believing in me and allowing me to pursue my dreams.

Chris Blewitt

ABOUT THE AUTHOR

This is Chris Blewitt's third publication. His first, *Deep Rough – A Thriller in Augusta*, is a thriller set in golf's grand stage, The Masters. *Deep Rough* has climbed the charts and has been the # 1 Sports, # 1 Golf, and # 1 Sports Gambling book on The Kindle.

Chris has also written the short story, *The Chemist – Based on a True Story.* Set in the 1920's, an innocent man is forced into the dangerous world of bootlegging during Prohibition.

Look for more from Chris in the coming months and learn more at www.chrisblewitt.com. Chris is always eager to hear from his fans, so feel free to drop him a line at: chris@chrisblewitt.com

Made in the USA
Lexington, KY
25 October 2018